ALASKAN RESCUE

TERRI REED

LOVE INSPIRED SUSPENSE
INSPIRATIONAL ROMANCE

Special thanks and acknowledgment are given to Terri Reed
for her contribution to the Alaska K-9 Unit miniseries.

LOVE INSPIRED® SUSPENSE

INSPIRATIONAL ROMANCE

Recycling programs
for this product may
not exist in your area.

ISBN-13: 978-1-335-72233-1

Alaskan Rescue

Copyright © 2021 by Harlequin Books S.A.

This edition published by arrangement with Harlequin Books S.A.

For questions and comments about the quality of this book, please contact us
at CustomerService@Harlequin.com.

Love Inspired
22 Adelaide St. West, 40th Floor
Toronto, Ontario M5H 4E3, Canada
www.Harlequin.com

Printed in U.S.A.

Now the God of hope fill you with all joy and peace
in believing, that ye may abound in hope,
through the power of the Holy Ghost.
—*Romans* 15:13

As always, it was such a pleasure to work with the other ladies, Maggie K. Black, Sharon Dunn, Laura Scott, Jodie Bailey, Heather Woodhaven, Dana Mentink, Shirlee McCoy and Lenora Worth. You all make the writing fun. And a big thank-you to our editor, Emily Rodmell, for guiding us along the way.

A special thank-you to Patricia Whitesell for all the lovely photos of your Siberian huskies and interesting details that helped to bring Juneau alive.

ONE

"Ariel, hurry up."

"Coming. Are we sure we should be doing this?" Ariel Potter glanced behind her. Nothing but trees and thick underbrush covered in layers of April snow.

When Ariel's best friend, Violet James, had called her this morning to announce they were going on yet another wedding party excursion, which included Violet's fiancé, Lance Wells, and his best man, Jared Dennis, Ariel had anticipated maybe they were going sledding or even skiing. Certainly not hiking in Chugach State Park through the snow-covered forested mountains, one of the many natural wonders of Alaska.

Their tour guide, Cal Brooks, had led them off the marked trail despite the signs clearly stating all hikers were to stay on the path. Anxiety fluttered in Ariel's stomach. They were breaking the rules, which wasn't cool.

"It's fine." Violet adjusted her sky-blue knit

cap over her medium-length blond hair. "You worry too much. We're going to lose the guys if we don't hurry."

Shaking her head, Ariel trudged on, thankful for the waterproof insulated boots on her feet. A shiver traipsed down her spine despite the warmth of her bright pink feather down jacket.

The area was so wild and remote, reminding her of the time when she was six and wandered from her family's campsite. It had been hours before she'd found her way back. Her parents hadn't even noticed her missing.

Her fingers curled against the memory. She was thankful for the hand warmers inside her gloves. The Nikon D7500 camera hanging around her neck had grown heavy. The thing only weighed a pound and a half but could be more like twenty if the pain tugging at her neck was any indication. She lifted it off her chest and snapped some pictures of Violet's retreating back and of the three men even farther ahead as they crested the rise and then moved out of sight.

With a sigh of resignation, Ariel continued to trek through the snow. This was not how she had wanted to spend her Saturday. She should be training her sled dogs for next weekend's last fun run race of the season. As well as seeing to the next breeding schedule, which was her main source of income.

And there was the puppy to consider. Poor Sasha was no doubt confused to be sent to the neighbors for the day again.

Not to mention, this week Ariel was going to be accepting an award for her skill at breeding champion dogs. The Iditarod had recently ended and many of her champion Alaskan husky sled dogs had placed in the top positions with their respective mushers, and she hadn't even started on her acceptance speech.

The only thing she could come up with was thanking her nomadic parents for teaching her everything she knew about dogs, mushing and breeding. Not that they would be in attendance. Her parents lived out of a travel trailer and rarely stayed in one place. It had been six months since the last time they'd stopped through Anchorage on their roamings.

Ah well. It was her own fault for letting Violet convince her that she could take a day off. Actually, another day in a long line of days off.

As the maid of honor, Ariel could hardly refuse Violet, who was so excited about her upcoming nuptials. Lance Wells, the groom-to-be, had planned all sorts of wedding events over the past week. First it had been whale watching, next an escape room adventure, then line dancing, and now hiking on unmarked trails.

Lance had insisted on this excursion and Violet seemed to want to do anything that Lance said. Because she was in love.

Ariel didn't like the sour grapes twisting in her chest. At twenty-nine, she kind of despaired she'd ever find her Mr. Right. She wasn't looking, mind you. Love seemed like a risky endeavor. Especially after the fiasco of her last boyfriend, Jason. A mistake she truly regretted. He'd seemed so sweet and kind at first, but then she'd realized it was a facade. She didn't care for the man he really was and had broken off their relationship.

But still, she liked the idea of a grand romance.

Up ahead, Violet crested the rise and disappeared.

With a grunt of frustration, Ariel stepped up her pace. She was honest enough with herself to realize she was a tad bit jealous, and sad, because she was losing another friend to marriage. Violet and Lance's wedding would be the fifth one that Ariel had been involved in over the past year and a half. What was it about nearing thirty that made people decide it was time to marry?

But Ariel really was happy for Violet. She was her best friend. And this was the first time she had been asked to be the maid of honor.

However, Ariel couldn't banish the deep sense of unease niggling at the back of her mind.

There was nothing specific that had her on

edge lately. Just this strange sensation that something dark lurked, waiting to strike.

Giving herself a mental head slap for her silly imagination, she crested the rise onto an outcrop that ran along the mountainside. As her boots crunched over the rocks beneath the layer of hard-packed snow, she noticed her hiking mates were already starting up the next incline, and that she'd lost sight of Violet among the thick forest. Uh-oh.

The altitude pulled at Ariel's lungs. Her breath came out in ragged puffs. Shielding her eyes from the overcast sky, she contemplated the next mountain. Really? They were going to hike up *that* now?

Making a face, she turned to look out over the vista, needing a moment before she hurried after her friends. From this vantage point she could see the majestic Denali mountain, the tallest in North America, and the sprawling city that was Anchorage. The place she called home.

Movement in the sky caught her attention. A bald eagle soared, its wings spread. The white tail and head were so bright in contrast to the bird's dark body. Though Alaska was home to the bald eagle, Ariel never tired of them.

Seeing the majestic bird reminded her of the verse in Isaiah that said, *"Those who hope in the Lord will renew their strength. They will soar on wings like eagles, they will run and not grow weary, they will walk and not be faint."*

She scrambled to lift her camera to take pictures. The eagle dipped lower. Ariel hurried along the outcrop to the very edge, where it narrowed, snapping off images as the bird dipped, clearly looking for dinner.

The loud bang of a gun echoed across the valley. Startled, Ariel shivered, but chalked the noise up to hunters. She deplored that the state park allowed the hunting of one black bear per hunter from September through May.

Refocusing on the eagle, Ariel continued to take snapshots as the bird dove below the tree line and out of sight. Staring down the side of the cliff made her dizzy. It was a long drop to the bottom with many trees and rocks dotting the landscape and jutting out of the side of the steep cliff.

A moment later the eagle swooped toward the sky with a hare dangling in its mouth. The bird turned in a big arc and headed right toward Ariel. Her heart stalled in her chest. These were going to be fabulous photos.

From behind her, the rush of footsteps made her wince. No doubt Violet coming to retrieve her wayward maid of honor.

As the eagle flew overhead, a hand on Ariel's back shoved her forward. Her feet lost traction.

She slipped off the edge of the cliff, her arms flaying, the camera banging against her chest. A scream escaped her and echoed in her ears.

Lord, please help me!

She tucked herself into a ball and hit the side of the cliff, her body rolling over sharp debris. The back of her head slammed against something hard. Pain exploded through her. She cried out, terrified that she was going to die.

Alaska State Trooper and K-9 handler Hunter McCord stepped into the conference room of the Alaska K-9 Unit headquarters late Saturday afternoon. Why had his boss, Colonel Lorenza Gallo, called a team meeting today? The unit typically had team briefings multiple times during the work week because Lorenza deemed it important that the team stay connected to one another and to the cases that were happening across the state of Alaska. But coming in on the weekend was unusual.

"All right everyone, settle down. Take a seat." Lorenza, wearing a tailored navy pantsuit sporting one of her signature elaborate gold and jewel-studded broaches on the lapel, stood at the front of the room. Beside her sat her senior dog, Denali, a handsome white-and-gray husky with bright blue eyes.

Tall and commanding with short silver hair,

the colonel had been one of the state's first female state troopers to work with a K-9 and had formed the Alaska K-9 Unit ten years ago as a specialty team comprised of K-9 state troopers to supplement the state's law enforcement reach, especially in rural areas without resources for any K-9 dogs.

Lorenza had recruited state troopers from across Alaska and provided a requisite twelve-week instruction course at the K-9 training center that the state troopers shared with the Metro police department, which was located directly behind the Anchorage headquarters.

Planting himself in the nearest chair, Hunter noticed Trooper Helena Maddox leaning against the wall. She and her partner, a Norwegian elk-hound named Luna, specialized in suspect apprehension.

Rising quickly, Hunter offered her the chair. When the whole team was assembled, they usually were short a couple of seats. "Here you go, Helena."

With a grateful smile, she slipped into the chair. "Thank you, Hunter."

"Of course." He noticed the dark circles under her green eyes. "You doing okay? You look stressed."

She shrugged. "I'm just worried about my sister. I haven't heard from her in a while and she's not returning my texts or calls."

Concerned, Hunter put his hand on her shoulder. When one team member hurt, they all did. They were a family. "Let me know if I can help."

"Thanks," she said. "I will."

Hunter moved to rest his shoulder against the wall beside Trooper Will Stryker. He was passionate about stopping the drug trade in the state and his partner, a border collie, excelled at detecting the illegal substances. "Hey."

Will, roughly the same height and build as Hunter, gave him the chin nod.

"Do you know what this is about?" Hunter asked, his voice low.

"No idea," Will replied, his brown eyes looking more serious than usual as he focused on their boss.

Trooper Sean West glanced over his shoulder from his seat next to Helena. "Something big must be happening."

Hunter hoped Sean and his cadaver-seeking partner, an Akita named Grace, wouldn't be called upon today. Recoveries were hard on all of them.

Lorenza held up a hand, quieting the room. "I know it's a Saturday and some of you are technically off. But crime does not rest."

There was a murmur of agreement through the room.

"Earlier this afternoon, the tour company, Unexplored Alaska, called Metro police when one of their tour guides and his group of four didn't return to base as scheduled. They were headed into Chugach State Park for an 'off the beaten path' hike. The police, accompanied by the owner of Unexplored Alaska, searched the area that was on the tour guide's agenda."

Lorenza taped up a photo onto the glass wall behind her of a young man lying prone in the snow. "The guide, Cal Brooks, was found dead from a single gunshot wound to the chest."

She put up four other images, which looked like driver's license pictures, onto the glass pane.

"The hikers were all part of a wedding party, consisting of the bride-to-be, Violet James." Lorenza pointed to a photo of a blonde woman with big blue eyes and delicate features. "Violet is the daughter of the late Alaskan oil baron Samuel James and his wife, Marie."

She gestured to the two men's images on the wall. "Her fiancé, Lance Wells, owns and operates an import-export business, and his best man, Jared Dennis, is a commercial fisherman. And the maid of honor, Ariel Potter, is a local Alaskan husky breeder." The last photo was of another blonde with pale brown eyes and a generous smile. "These four are missing. No trace of them. The local PD has requested our help."

"Could this be a kidnapping?" Trooper Brayden Ford asked. "Was the deceased found near one of the lakes in the park?"

Brayden and his partner, a Newfoundland named Ella, handled the team's underwater searches.

"No body of water nearby. As for kidnapping, that remains to be seen."

"Have there been any avalanches reported?" Trooper Gabriel Runyon asked from the other side of the conference table. Gabriel and his beautiful Saint Bernard, Bear, were proficient in avalanche detection.

"None reported in that area, but if you would work with the state's avalanche technician and see if there has been any activity in the park, that would be helpful," Lorenza said. "At this point we don't have enough information to know the motive for the murder. We need to know what happened to these four civilians and who killed the tour guide and why." Her gaze swept over the room and landed on Hunter. "Hunter."

Under Lorenza's scrutiny, he straightened from the wall. "Yes, ma'am."

"You will lead a search team. Maya and Poppy will go with you."

Grateful for the opportunity to take point on

the search, Hunter kept his satisfaction in check. He would do his colonel proud.

"See Katie on your way out," Lorenza continued. "She will give you the details." Her steel-eyed gaze returned to the room at large. "The rest of you, I want in-depth background checks on all five of these people. Was Cal Brooks involved in criminal activity that followed him up the mountain? Or was one of the others the target? And we will work with the James family in case this is a kidnapping and ransom demands are made."

Mentally going through his checklist of equipment needed, Hunter headed for the conference room door, along with fellow troopers Maya Rodriguez and Poppy Walsh.

In the hallway, he paused. "I'll meet you two and your partners at Katie's desk," Hunter said. "Gear up. We're in for more snow."

"Roger that." Poppy pushed back her auburn-colored bangs. "I wonder if the tour group happened upon poachers?"

"A valid question considering the state park's hunting restrictions," Hunter said.

Which was probably why the colonel assigned Poppy and Stormy, an Irish wolfhound, for the initial deploy. Stormy was highly cross-trained to detect weapons and people, while Poppy was also an experienced wildlife trooper. Maya and her partner, a Malinois name Sarge, were experts at sniffing out all types of weapons and explosives. Even infectious diseases.

After retrieving his partner, a red-and-white Siberian husky named Juneau, from Hunter's assigned small office and gathering the equipment necessary for a mountain search, Hunter headed to the colonel's administrative assistant's office. He stopped in the doorway.

"Good afternoon, Hunter. Come in," Katie Kapowski, a petite redhead with sharp green eyes, was the consummate professional. She rose from her desk with a file folder in her hand.

As Maya and Poppy and their respective dogs joined Hunter and Juneau, Katie gave Hunter the folder. "Here's everything I could gather quickly on the missing wedding party. I've already been fielding calls from Mrs. James and her representatives, wanting answers."

"We will do our best to bring home the four missing people," Hunter assured her. He never made promises he couldn't keep, and he knew from experience that sometimes search and rescue missions ended up as recoveries. He sent up a prayer that wouldn't be the case here.

Following the directions in the file folder, Hunter drove his vehicle to the Glen Alps trailhead parking area. Poppy and Maya brought their own SUVs to a halt alongside his.

A Metro police cruiser sat waiting with its motor running next to a van with the logo of the tour company, Unexplored Alaska.

Hunter climbed out of his SUV and breathed in the crisp, cold air. Overhead more clouds gathered, giving credence to the predicted coming snowfall.

A tall police officer climbed out of the cruiser and jogged over to him. "Trooper McCord?" the officer asked.

Hunter stuck out his hand. "Yes. Hunter McCord. Officer—" Hunter glanced at the name badge on the other man's jacket. "Brand."

"Call me Everett. My chief wanted me to let you look at the Unexplored Alaska van before we have it taken to the state crime lab."

"I appreciate it," Hunter said. "Were there any signs of foul play in or around the van?"

"Not that we saw," Everett said. "But I'm sure Tala will find anything if there is something to find."

Hunter knew the forensic tech, Tala Ekho, from the Alaska State Crime Lab, was top-notch, and he had confidence that what Everett said was true.

"Open the van, will you?" Hunter instructed. "We'll let the dogs take a good sniff."

Everett complied, opening the side door to the ten-passenger cargo van.

After releasing Juneau from his compartment in the SUV, Hunter had the dog explore the van. Then Hunter and Juneau moved aside to let Maya and Sarge take a sniff. Then Poppy and Stormy had a turn. Though Sarge and Stormy weren't necessarily trained for search and rescue, their noses would be assets out in the field.

Everett locked up the van when they were done.

"We're going to head up the mountain and search for our missing wedding party," Hunter told him. "If we find anything, I'll alert dispatch and they can alert you."

"Copy," Everett said and jogged back to his cruiser.

Consulting the notes provided by Katie, Hunter said to Poppy and Maya, "We take the main trail, and then we'll branch off to an alternate route for the top of Flattop Mountain."

"Where was the tour guide found?" Maya asked, looking over his shoulder at the map.

"Here." He pointed to a red dot that had been marked on the paper topography map. "A few yards above what looks like a crag in the mountainside."

"Let's do this," Poppy said as she adjusted the strap on her climbing helmet.

Hunter tucked the map into the front zippered pocket of his winterized jacket. He put his climbing helmet on his head, making sure his goggles had a good seal before jamming his hands into his gloves. Then he hefted his internal frame pack loaded with everything he could possibly need for this mission onto his back.

Maya and Poppy also had similar packs. And the dogs were outfitted with winter coats marked Alaska K-9 Unit and long leads.

Hunter and Juneau led the way up the marked trail at a fast clip. When he gauged they'd traveled the right distance, he checked the map again, looking for where the tour guide had taken his party off the path.

Maya and Sarge moved ahead of Hunter. "Here." She gestured to where a yellow cone had been set in the snow, revealing the route many feet had recently tread, which appeared to lead toward Flattop.

With Maya now leading the way, they followed the intermittent yellow cones as they traversed the manmade footpath. The terrain was rough, the forest thick and the incline steep.

"We're coming to the crag," Hunter said loudly.

The outcrop was approximately ten feet wide where they stood but extended farther along the face of the mountain until it narrowed into a short ledge, barely wide enough to stand on.

More yellow cones led up the next incline.

Hunter paused to assess the area. There were footprints in the snow all over the outcrop. No doubt from the tour group and the police department.

"Let's spread out," he said. "Maya, search where the body was discovered. See if you can find the weapon or any other evidence that might be useful."

Maya nodded. Then she and Sarge proceeded to follow the cones.

Hunter stood facing the mountain. "The others had to go up, right?"

"Or around," Poppy said. "There was nothing to suggest they went back the way they came."

"You take a path up to the right," Hunter suggested. "I'll go to the left. Check in frequently."

"You got it." Poppy and Stormy headed off.

Hunter unhooked Juneau from his lead. "Search."

The dog cocked his head, sniffed the air, then put his nose to the snow. Rather than turning toward the trees as Hunter expected, the dog took off toward the place on the outcrop that was narrow. Juneau stared over the side of the cliff, let out a series of sharp howls, then hurried back to Hunter before circling back to the edge of the cliff.

Hunter rushed forward. He peered over the side but couldn't see anything through the thick forest and snow covering the side of the mountain. He shrugged off his pack and retrieved his binoculars. Once he had them adjusted properly, he swept his gaze looking for what had Juneau alerting.

His gaze snagged on a flash of bright pink.

There was someone caught on a large bramble growing out of the side of cliff face about twenty feet below where he stood. He was going to have to rappel down the mountain.

He prayed this was a rescue and not a recovery.

TWO

Heart beating a chaotic rhythm in his chest with his gaze locked on the still figure sprawled in the snow-dusted bushes below, Hunter grabbed the radio from beneath his jacket. Thumbing the mic, he said, "Poppy, Maya, I found one of the wedding party over the edge of the outcrop. I need to get down there."

"Headed back now," Poppy's voice came through the device.

"Copy," Maya said. "On our way."

Hunter took another look through the binoculars and stared down at the motionless form. The bright pink of the jacket suggested a female. Her blond hair was matted with blood on the back of her head. The bride or her bridesmaid?

The grooves in the snow suggested she tumbled down the side of the cliff.

Dead or alive? His gut twisted. It had been three hours since the wedding party had gone missing. If the woman below was alive, she had no doubt sustained injuries and was probably slipping into hypothermia.

Hunter had to get to her.

Using the radio again, he called dispatch, asking for EMS. He gave them the location. Then he searched through his pack and unloaded the rappelling gear, which consisted of ropes, a climbing harness, and a carabiner brake rig. Spying a nearby tree that would be a sturdy anchor, he looped the ropes around the tree trunk, then made a bowline removal knot. He tugged on the rope, assuring the knot would hold, then stretched the ropes to the edge of the cliff. Once he had his harness secured around his waist, Hunter threaded one end of each rope though his Rollnlock, an ultra-light pulley and rope clamp/brake.

Poppy and Stormy came out of the trees, dislodging clumps of snow from the branches, and hurried over. Poppy gave the command for Stormy to sit. The big Irish wolfhound's head almost reached her shoulder.

"I called for EMS," Hunter said, handing her the binoculars.

Poppy went to the edge of the cliff, then hustled back to his side. "I see her."

"I tied off to the tree as an anchor," he informed her. "I need you to keep the lines from tangling and make sure the ropes don't get caught on anything."

"Will do."

Within moments, Maya and Sarge joined them. Snow clung to Sarge's fur. Hunter explained his plan to rappel down the side of the mountain to assess the woman's injuries.

"Maya, can you be my beta and navigate me down?"

"With pleasure." Taking the binoculars, Maya hurried to the cliff's edge and lay down so she could peer over the side. Sarge went on his belly beside her.

Hunter secured his goggles, slipped on his heavy-duty climbing gloves, then double-checked his harness and rigging.

After a moment of scanning the trees, Maya said, "Okay, you're going to go straight down from here. Then you'll need to go twenty degrees to your left to miss a boulder. It appears to have a smear of blood on it."

"Got it," Hunter replied. "That explains the blood on our victim's head." He didn't like the idea of a head injury.

"Ropes look good," Poppy said.

To Juneau, Hunter said, "Down." The dog went onto his belly. "Stay."

Hunter knew his K-9 partner wouldn't break until given permission. There was no reason to take Juneau down the face of the cliff. "Poppy, can you send word to Sean that a search around the base of the mountain is in order in case any other wedding party members also went over the side of this ledge and weren't as blessed to have a bush break their descent?"

Sean and Grace would recover whomever hadn't survived the fall because the base of the mountain was a good sixty or so feet down. Hunter sent up a prayer that the victim he was about to rappel to would be alive.

At the edge of the crag, after one last safety check of his harnesses and then locking the carabiner clip that would act as a brake, Hunter clutched the rope and put his booted feet on the lip of the ledge, bracing himself as he leaned back and stretched his legs out. Slowly he walked his way down the cliff face, allowing the rope to slide smoothly through the device. His boots slipped on loose rock and debris beneath the layer of snow, but thankfully, they were equipped with crampons that provided traction.

With each step of his descent, his heart stuttered. Questions ran through his mind. Who shot the tour guide? And why? Was this a kidnapping gone wrong? Or something else? Was the woman below alive?

He paused a moment to glance upward as the

first few flakes of snow began to fall, quickly melting against his jacket.

A sense of urgency hurried him on, and he quickened his pace.

"Stop!" Maya called. "Shift left."

Praying the rope didn't fray on the sharp edge of the outcrop, he walked horizontally along the sheer cliff face.

"Perfect," Maya said. "Good to go for ten more feet."

Moving swiftly yet carefully, Hunter glanced over his shoulder. He was almost to the woman. Her blond hair was tangled in the branches of the bush she'd landed on. He grimaced at the up close sight of matted blood on the back of her head.

Thankfully, the thicket had prevented her from falling farther down the mountainside. Hunter sent a quick praise to God for big blessings.

When he reached the woman's side, he planted his feet to brace himself, locked his brake mechanism in place and then stripped one glove off.

He gauged the woman's height around five feet, six inches. She wore hiking boots and snow pants and gloves.

Careful not to dislodge her, he rooted beneath her hair and the collar of her bright pink coat for her neck, praying he would find a pulse.

There was a definite thump against his finger. A pulse. Weak, but there. "Yes!"

Where were her friends? Was this the bride?

Hunter thumbed his mic on his radio. "The woman is alive. As soon as EMS arrives, we need a litter down here," he said. "I don't want to move her until we have to."

Poppy's voice crackled on the radio. "EMS is on their way to us. I will let them know the status of our rescue."

A *rescue*. Hunter once again sent up a praise to God for another blessing on this bleak day. The irony that he was thanking his Heavenly Father wasn't lost on Hunter. There had been too many prayers that had gone unanswered over the years.

A groan echoed in Ariel's ears. Was someone hurt? She needed to help them.

She heard another moan and decided she was the source of the noise. Nausea rolled through her stomach as the world seemed to spin. What was happening?

Somewhere in her mind, she realized she was being turned over onto a hard surface. Dull pain pounded the back of her head.

"Miss? Miss?"

A hand on her shoulder brought Ariel out of the foggy state engulfing her. Opening her eyelids proved to be a struggle. Snow fell from the sky, stinging her cheeks, falling into her eyes. Then a hand shielded her face from the elements.

Her gaze passed across broad shoulders to a very handsome face beneath a helmet. Dark hair peeked out from the edge of the helmet and a pair of goggles hung from his neck. Was she dreaming? Who was this man?

She'd never seen this guy before in her life. This had to be a dream, right? Yet how could she dream about a man she'd never seen before?

The pull of sleep was hard to resist. She closed her eyes. Maybe the man in her dream would help her. But help her with what?

"Stay with me," the man murmured.

His voice coaxed her to do as he instructed, and she forced her eyes open.

Where was she?

Awareness of aches and pains screamed throughout her body, bringing the world into sharp focus. She was flat on her back and her head throbbed.

Ariel started to raise a hand to touch her head, but something was holding her arm down. She tried to sit up, and when she discovered she couldn't, she lifted her head to see why. Though doing so created more pain. Straps had been placed across her shoulders, her torso, hips and knees to keep her in place on a rescue basket. A metallic silver Mylar blanket had been tucked around her, insulating her body's warmth.

"Hey, now, I need you to concentrate on being still and staying awake."

That deep, rich voice brought her focus back to the moment. Memory flooded her on a wave of terror. The horror of rolling down the side of the cliff, hitting her head, landing in a bramble bush, and the fear of moving that would take her plummeting to the bottom of the mountain. She must have gone in and out of consciousness before being rescued. She gasped with realization. "Someone pushed me!"

The handsome man's piercing blue eyes widened. Then his eyebrows drew together. "*Pushed* you?"

"Where's Violet? Lance and Jared?" She struggled not to freak out. Why had someone shoved her off the edge of the cliff?

The man winced slightly. "You're safe now. No one's going to hurt you."

Her dream man's voice soothed her. But why wasn't he answering her questions? She swallowed, her mind rebelling at the possible answers. "Who are you?"

"Trooper Hunter McCord."

Definitely not someone she'd previously met. Ariel rolled the name around in her head. She liked the sound of it. Strong consonants, masculine and powerful. Was he someone she could count on? Trust?

Doubtful, her cynical side chimed in. There was no one she could rely on in life, except for God. She knew this, but still that dream of a grand romance lingered at the edges of her consciousness. Hmm. She must've taken a hard hit to the head if she was romanticizing her rescuer.

A beam of light shone bright in her eyes. "Can you tell us your name?"

She flinched against the light. "Ariel Potter."

When the light was turned off, she realized the first man wasn't alone. Two other men were with him, both dressed in snow coveralls with the Anchorage Emergency Medical Services logo on the breast pocket and across their helmets.

The men talked in a low tone with the trooper. She couldn't make out the words though she strained to hear.

Hunter moved closer. "Okay, Ariel, we're going to lift the rescue basket and take you up the side of the mountain."

"What?" She writhed against the restraints.

"Don't move," Hunter said again. "It'll be a lot easier on everybody if you lie still and let the EMS do their job."

She settled down, trying to keep her body still. She hated the helpless, vulnerable reaction stealing over her.

Hunter straightened. He made a whirling motion with his hand. And then she was moving. First, she was elevated to only a slight incline, and then she was almost vertical as the basket was pulled up the side of the cliff. Her stomach lurched, and her heart slammed against her ribs. She watched the world through narrowed eyes, too afraid to close her eyes but too afraid to open them all the way.

Beside her, Hunter climbed alongside the basket.

It seemed like forever before she was horizontal again.

Once the basket was no longer moving, a wet, rough tongue licked her hand. She jerked, her gaze locking eyes with a dog. A beautiful rust-and-white-colored Siberian husky with amber-colored eyes that seemed to express worry. *For her?* Why would a dog she'd never met be concerned about her? Was the dog even real?

A woman squatted down next to her. She had auburn hair and a kind smile. Her jacket was similar to Hunter's with the words Alaska State Trooper K-9 Unit. "I'm Poppy."

"Where is Violet? Please, you have to tell me."

"We're working on finding your friends," Poppy said. "Right now you need to concentrate on you. You took a nasty spill. Let us worry about them."

Ariel's mouth dried as the trooper's words sank in. Something was wrong. Panic assailed her, and she bucked on the litter beneath her. A strong hand gripped her shoulder, forcing her to turn her head away from the woman. She met Hunter's piercing blue eyes once again.

"You're going to injure yourself," he said, concern etched in the lines of his face. "Your friends are our priority. We'll keep searching for them, but we need to get you to the hospital."

She shook her head, wincing at the cascade of pain that rippled over her. "No, you need to find them now. Find Violet. You don't understand, she's—" Ariel clamped her lips together. That wasn't her secret to tell.

Hunter frowned. "She's what?"

Ariel hesitated but then decided they needed to know. "Violet's pregnant. Please, you have to find her."

Surprise flashed across Hunter's face. He turned to Poppy. "Can you update the colonel?"

"Of course." Poppy moved away to talk on her radio.

Hunter refocused on Ariel. "You said somebody pushed you?"

"Yes." She took a shuddering breath. "I was taking pictures of a bald eagle. Oh, no, my camera!"

Hunter held up her Nikon. The outside casing

was cracked with pieces missing, and the lens had fractured into a spiderweb of lines. "I found it. It's pretty banged up. Sad to say you'll need a new one. I'll put it in my bag."

She sighed, part frustration, part relief. "Thank you."

"You were saying…?" he prompted.

Refocusing took effort. "I heard a noise, like someone running toward me, and then—" Her voice broke. "Someone pushed me."

Her heart sank. Had one of her friends done this? No. She couldn't believe that. *Wouldn't* believe it. Someone else must've come up behind her at the edge of the outcrop. She should have stayed with her friends. Why hadn't they come looking for her? "Did Violet call you?" She couldn't keep the hope out of her voice. "Is that why you came to find me?"

Hunter shook his head. "I'm sorry, no. Do you know where your friends went?"

She turned her head toward the mountain. "Up there." When she looked back at Hunter, she caught the glance he exchanged with a dark-haired woman who was rolling up a length of rope.

Three dogs sat in a line, staring at Ariel. She blinked, half afraid they would disappear, but the dogs remained. The beautiful Siberian husky, an Irish wolfhound and a Malinois. Each wore a vest with the words Alaska State Trooper K-9 Unit stitched into the fabric. So well trained.

Ariel missed her own dogs. The need to return to her pack brought tears to her eyes.

"Did the tour guide lead your friends up the mountain?" Hunter's question brought her focus back to him.

Unease traipsed down Ariel's spine. "He did. He said we were going on an untraveled trail. The tour guide was supposed to keep us safe. Is he missing, too?"

Hunter's expression darkened. "There'll be time enough for all of this later, but right now we have to get you to the ambulance waiting at the parking lot."

The two EMS men moved to the front and back of the basket. "We'll carry her."

Hunter straightened. "The snow is packed well enough we can hook the basket up to the dogs. They can transport her to the parking lot."

"Are your dogs used to sleds?" Ariel asked. Having trained sled dogs her whole life, she knew it wasn't as simple as hooking a dog to a sled and expecting the animal to know how to safely pull a sled, or rescue basket, in this case.

Hunter's head tilted. "All our dogs are properly trained."

She bit her lip to keep from directing him as he and the other two troopers attached lines to the basket, then produced the proper nylon harnesses for the three canines. She couldn't fault their work.

Within a short time, the dogs were hooked to the basket with the Siberian husky up front taking the lead position, then the Malinois doing double duty as the swing and team dog with the Irish wolfhound as the wheel.

Hunter gave the command prompting the dogs to pull. "Let's go."

With the humans walking on each side of Ariel, the dogs carted her down the mountain. While the going was mostly smooth across the snow, the occasional bump sent pain stabbing through her head. When they arrived at the parking lot, an ambulance waited and she was transferred to the bay of the vehicle. The two emergency medical service men consulted with the ambulance personnel before heading to their own rig.

"How did you find me?" Ariel asked Hunter as he and his dog stood by the ambulance doors.

Hunter put his hand on the dog's back. "Juneau found you. He's a—"

"Siberian husky," she said at the same time he did.

Hunter smiled. He had a nice smile. "Yes."

"Sir, we need to go," the paramedic said as he climbed in beside Ariel.

"Wait! Please, Hunter, tell me what happened to my friends."

There was a brief hesitation before he said, "They're missing."

Ariel's heart clenched. "What about the tour guide?"

Hunter's gaze darkened. "He was shot and killed."

The breath left her lungs.

"Do you know why someone would want to kill you?"

"I don't know." Tears burned her eyes.

"We'll have to assume that whoever did this will try again once they learn you're still alive."

His words sent terror streaking through her heart. But why would someone want her dead?

THREE

Hunter hooked his thumbs in his uniform utility belt and paced outside the emergency exam room of Alaska Regional Hospital, waiting for the doctor to finish his examination of Ariel Potter. Juneau sat by the door as if guarding the entrance.

Why had someone pushed Ariel off the edge of the cliff? Where were the other wedding party members? Who shot the tour guide?

The questions bounced around Hunter's head, unanswerable and not nearly distracting enough.

Everything about hospitals made him twitchy. The beeping of the monitors shuddered through him like alarm bells, and the smells of disinfectant and sickness turned his stomach. Anxiety clawed its way up his spine, an all-too-familiar sensation that brought back dreadful memories. Memories he'd rather not relive.

Yet with every passing second, he was taken back to age twelve. His mother had been diagnosed with stage IV pancreatic cancer. There'd been many doctor visits, trips to the ER, and hospital stays. Hunter had considered those days would be the worst he'd ever have to face, crying out to God to save his mother.

God hadn't saved his mother. She had passed with her husband and son by her side.

His father had done the best he could as a widower raising a rambunctious teen on his own while serving the community as a Metro police officer. Hunter had followed in his father's footsteps by going into law enforcement.

Then, five years ago, Kenneth McCord had been retired and restless until he'd met Celeste Roper, who, it turned out, was involved with a scam ring. Celeste had fleeced his father of his life savings. With some good detective work, she and the ring had been brought down and now were in prison.

And God had denied Hunter's request to save his father from the danger of a ruthless woman, which left him wary of God and His promises. Why had God let his mother die and his father lose his life savings?

The swish of the sliding glass door opening yanked Hunter from his spiraling thoughts, and he straightened as the doctor walked out. Juneau stepped inside the doorway as if to see what was happening inside the exam room. Hunter let out a short whistle, bringing the dog back to heel.

Hunter strode over to Dr. Chen. The doctor had been working at the hospital for as long as he could remember. He was a tall, lanky man with a headful of thick salt and pepper hair and dark eyes.

"How's the patient?"

Dr. Chen said, "Miss Potter is a little banged up, though nothing is broken and there are no major internal injuries. She did take a blow to the head and will need to be monitored closely for the next twenty-four hours. I didn't see anything abnormal on the CT scan, and she's lucid. I've made her promise to follow up with her primary care doctor."

"I'll make sure someone is with her around the clock," Hunter promised. Surely Ariel had family who would be willing to come to stay with her overnight.

Curiosity burned in the doctor's eyes. "You don't normally wait around to check on those you bring to the hospital."

"Miss Potter is part of an active investigation," Hunter replied.

Ariel had to know something that would help the Alaska K-9 Unit uncover what had happened on the mountain. That she was pretty and vulnerable and had sent all of his protective instincts surging really wasn't the point.

He had learned the hard way that pretty and

sweet didn't always reflect what went on inside a woman's heart.

Though he'd never questioned his mother's love for him, she'd been a hard woman to please. Combined with what happened to his father and Hunter's own dismal track record in the romance department, he had determined romance wasn't something he intended to pursue again. He had his faith, his father, Juneau and his family within the K-9 Unit. They were all he needed.

"It's not usual to see you taking an active interest in your witness," Dr. Chen said.

Hunter cocked his head. "Why assume she's a witness?" Had she said something to the doc that he needed to know?

Dr. Chen smiled. "You didn't put her in handcuffs. So either she's a witness, or—" His dark eyes assessed him. "You're worried about her."

There was truth in the doctor's words even if he didn't want to admit he was worried. "Someone hurt her. I want to make sure they don't succeed a second time."

"Very commendable."

"Just doing my job. I still need her official statement," Hunter said. "Can I see her?"

"I'll release her to your care," Dr. Chen said. "The nurse is helping her dress now. We gave her a pair of scrubs because her clothes were so tattered. And I figured you might want them for trace evidence. Though we did give her dry socks and put her boots back on to keep her feet warm."

"Thank you. That will be helpful. I'll have someone come retrieve them."

Dr. Chen shrugged. "You work emergency room trauma long enough, you know the drill. I'll have her discharge papers ready in a moment." He walked away.

A few seconds later the door to the exam room opened again and the curtain was pulled back. A young nurse wheeled Ariel from the room. She was dressed in green scrubs and cocooned in a thin blanket, clutching a brown paper bag in her hands. Hunter's gaze zeroed in on the bandage wrapped around Ariel's head, her blond hair sticking out like golden pieces of straw. Her cheeks were rosy, but her skin chalky, and the pupils of her pale brown eyes were dilated. She was still recovering from the shock of the fall. Juneau moved to walk beside Ariel's wheelchair.

When the nurse brought the chair to a halt, Juneau put his head on Ariel's knee. She stared at him while gently stroking his head. Hunter wasn't surprised that Juneau was offering her his comfort. The breed was highly intelligent, friendly and gentle. Juneau's gift of being in tune with the emotions of humans matched well with search and rescue work.

"She can take some Tylenol for the head-ache," Dr. Chen said, drawing Hunter's focus as he joined them and handed him paperwork with instructions. "If she worsens or blacks out, bring her back to the ER."

"You have my word," Hunter assured the doctor.

Shrugging out of his jacket, he gave it to Ariel. "Here, put this on."

She slipped her arms into the sleeves. The jacket was huge on her, but it would be warmer than the blanket.

"You're very kind," she murmured.

The nurse wheeled Ariel out to Hunter's SUV parked in the spot near the entrance reserved for law enforcement. The night was dark, broken only by the glow of the streetlamps. Snow continued to fall steadily, coating the world in pristine white.

Ariel glanced up at him, blinking away the snowflakes landing on her eyelashes. "You don't have to take me home. You can just put me in a cab."

"Not happening, Miss Potter," Hunter said. "Someone tried to kill you. Your friends are missing, and a man is dead."

Her shoulders slumped. "I know. You don't have to remind me. You should be out looking for my friends."

"People are searching for them now."

"Why are you helping me?" The genuine puzzlement in her tone had him frowning. Why did she find it strange that he'd want to assist her?

"Because you need help and it's my job."

"Ah. Well, thank you."

Her words made Hunter bristle. Yes, he was being paid to do his job, but he was also helping because she needed it and he could offer it. He assisted her into the front passenger seat, tucking the blanket around her and securing the seat belt in place. His jacket was big and bulky on her, making her appear young and vulnerable and in need of his protection. Part of his job was to protect, but what stirred the soft places in his chest had more to do with the woman than his duty as a law enforcement officer.

Uncomfortable with that notion, he put Juneau in his compartment, then jogged around to the driver's side and climbed in.

Ariel had opened the brown bag and retrieved her cell phone, which appeared intact. A frown pulled at her eyebrows. Her lower lip quivered.

"Everything okay?" he asked.

"Just texts asking to buy one of my pack dogs," she said.

He understood the value of canine companions, but he wasn't well versed in the monetary gain to be had from sled dogs. "Does that happen often?"

"I have at least three or four requests a week. I've told this particular person no several times, that I'm not interested in selling my breeding dogs, only the puppies," she said. "I was hoping maybe Violet had contacted me. I'm going to send her a text." She typed on the phone's keyboard.

The need to sooth away her troubles tugged at him, but at the moment, the most he could do was get her home and settled comfortably.

After starting the engine and turning the heat to high, he brought up the navigation system on his dashboard. "I need your address." Though he had it in the information Katie had given him, he'd rather engage Ariel.

She seemed to shake off whatever she was ruminating about to give him the street name and number. He typed it into the system. She lived on the outskirts of town. It made sense for a dog breeder to have a bit more space. The drive through Anchorage was quiet this late in the evening. The falling snow required the wipers to go full blast, the swishing noise grating on his nerves.

"Do you have someone to stay the night with you? Family I can call? A friend?"

She shook her head and winced. With a belea-guered sigh, she said, "No."

"No?" How could she not have family or friends?

"I'd say Violet, but… I suppose I could ask my neighbor if she'd be willing." Ariel blew out a breath. "I just hate to ask more from her. She has my puppy right now."

"Just one puppy?" Hunter loved all dogs. "I remember the joy, and misery, of taking care of a puppy. When I was a kid, my dad brought home an eight-week-old Lab. I loved that dog."

"Is that why you joined the K-9 Unit?" Her voice was soft and wrapped around him within the cab of the SUV.

"Yes. Raising Kato was the catalyst to me be-coming a K-9 handler."

"I imagine Juneau was a ball of fluff as a pup."

"I received Juneau as my partner when he was a year old. I missed out on the early development stage. And the sharp puppy teeth."

She laughed, the sound pleasing and melodic. "Yes, that is one of the hazards of raising pup-pies. Sasha, the puppy my neighbor is watch-ing, was the runt of my most recent litter and sickly. I had to nurse him to health. Most breed-ers would've let nature take its course or sold him as a pet. But I just couldn't do either. I fell in love with him."

"Puppies have that effect," he commented.

"I need to call my neighbor and check on Sasha. And make sure that Trevor fed the dogs. They are on a very regimented diet."

She rubbed at her forehead, clearly suffering a headache. Then she dialed and waited a moment. "Mrs. Nelson, it's Ariel. Everything is fine now. I took a fall on a hike today."

Hunter raised an eyebrow at her. Way to sugarcoat the incident.

"A little bruised," Ariel hedged. "How's Sasha?" She listened for a moment, then said, "I wouldn't want to burden you. Could you have Trevor bring him over to the house in about ten minutes…?" The conversation went on for a little while longer, and then once she'd confirmed that Trevor had in fact fed the dogs their dinner, she said goodbye and hung up.

"Who's Trevor?" Hunter asked.

"Mrs. Nelson's college-age son. Trevor's a responsible young man who will one day be a great musher and dog trainer. A few years ago he asked me to teach him how to mush. We worked out an agreement. I'd mentor him, but he also had to learn how to train dogs and help me around the kennel. A musher is only as good as the dogs pulling the sled."

He admired her compassion and commitment to her dogs. "Are you sure you're up for dealing with a puppy tonight?"

"Sasha is my responsibility," she said. "I'll be fine."

"Tell me about your breeding business."

She leaned her head back, then abruptly sat forward. No doubt putting pressure on the wound reminded her of her injury. Her hands twisted in her lap. "I breed Alaskan huskies. I took over the business from my father after college. My parents had run a smaller operation. But it was enough for us to get by on."

"Aren't the Alaskan huskies part Siberian husky?"

"The Alaskan husky isn't its own distinct breed but rather a mix of various northern breeds such as the Siberian, greyhound or German shorthaired pointer, and bred primarily to be working sled dogs. Most of my dogs were sired by one of my father's original dogs, Thorn. He was a mix of malamute and saluki. He was the best dog and sired a lot of champion sled dogs over the years. He passed not long after this last litter was born. I kept Sasha as a tribute to Thorn."

"How many dogs do you have?" Hunter asked.

"At the moment, nine including the puppy. I compete in smaller races with them in an effort to show off their abilities. People see how well they do and want their offspring. We have a race coming up the Sunday after Violet's wedding."

She gave a sigh filled with despair. "You will find her, won't you?"

"We won't rest until we do," he assured her. "Tell me about your friends."

"Violet and I were college roommates. She became my best friend even though our lives are so very different. She's kind and generous."

"What do you know about her fiancé?"

"He owns his own business. Violet met Lance at the golf club. Violet's mother doesn't exactly approve of Lance."

"Interesting. What's your take on him?"

There was a moment of silence before she said, "Violet is happy with Lance. That's all that matters to me."

Hunter had the sense there was something she wasn't saying. Did she not approve of Lance, too? Did Violet know this?

He brought his vehicle to a halt in front of her house. A ranch-style with two outbuildings and a large pasture rimmed by dark woods.

Ariel popped open her door. A cacophony of dogs howling echoed through the night.

In the dome light of the cab of his vehicle, her panic was visible. "Something's wrong!"

"They probably heard the crunch of the tires on the drive," Hunter said, praying that was the case.

"No. This is not normal." She jumped out.

Hunter hurried to her side and let Juneau out.

The dog sniffed the air and then growled. He took off at a fast run toward the closest outbuilding.

They rushed after Juneau.

A light glowed through the high windows along the side of the structure.

Ariel grabbed Hunter's arm. "Someone's in the kennels. My dogs are in trouble." She ran past him toward the building.

Adrenaline pumping through his veins, Hunter quickly caught up to her at the entrance door and kept her from touching it. The lock had been jimmied.

Tugging her behind him, he commanded, "Hang back."

He withdrew his sidearm and held the piece in a two-handed grip at the ready as he toed open the door. His ears were assaulted with the ferocious barking of the dogs.

At the far end of the kennel, a person dressed all in black had muzzled a dog and was attempting to drag the canine out of its kennel.

"No!" Ariel yelled and tried to push past Hunter, but Juneau blocked her.

"Halt, police!" Hunter shouted.

The intruder swung the beam of a flashlight in their direction, momentarily blinding Hunter, but not before he glimpsed the glint of a silver handgun tucked in the thief's waistband.

Abandoning what was clearly an attempted

theft, the perpetrator turned and bolted for the back door of the kennel building, escaping into the night.

Hunter pivoted with Juneau at his side and ran around the outside of the building. Then he abruptly stopped, unwilling to leave Ariel alone to chase after the suspect. He could barely discern the dark figure running away from Ariel's place through the open field toward the woods beyond. A few moments later an engine turned over. The armed suspect had escaped.

"Quiet," Ariel shouted as she quickly flipped on the overhead light switch. Her heart thumped in her chest so hard she hoped she didn't crack a rib. The fatigue she'd suffered in the car on the way home had evaporated to be replaced with anxious adrenaline.

The dogs immediately ceased their howling at her stern command. Each sat in its kennel, ears back and tail high. A quick glance at each assured her all but Dash in the last crate appeared unharmed.

She raced to the far end of the building and dropped to her knees inside Dash's open crate. He was a beautiful Alaskan husky with a blue-gray and white coat. A muzzle had been strapped in place over his nose and mouth. He lay on his side.

"Shh," Ariel soothed him. "It's okay. I'm here."

She undid the muzzle and stroked his thick coat. "What did that bad person do to you?" She ran her hands over the dog but found no obvious injuries.

Hunter and Juneau returned. Juneau whined and sat down next to Ariel.

"Is he okay?" Hunter asked as he crouched beside her.

"There's no physical injury that I can see," she said. "But he's groggy." She rose. Hunter followed suit.

"I need to call Cora," she said. Worry for her dogs made her limbs quake.

"Dr. Madison?"

"Yes. Do you know her?"

"She's the veterinarian the K-9 Unit uses."

Ariel wasn't surprised. "She's the best in the area."

"I have her on speed dial," Hunter said. He made the call and Cora promised to come right away. "She advises not moving Dash in case there are internal injuries. She said the best you can do is keep him quiet and still."

The thought of Dash hurting brought tears to Ariel's eyes.

Grateful to know help was on the way for her dog, she said, "I take it the intruder got away."

Hunter nodded. "I've called for backup."

Ariel shivered and burrowed deeper into the

trooper's jacket as the cold seeped through the thin scrubs. The scent of his spicy aftershave clinging to the fabric was pleasant and soothing. But still, a lump rose to her throat and she sniffed back tears in an attempt to keep them from spilling down her cheeks.

"Hey, now." Hunter gathered her in his arms. "You're safe. Your dogs are safe."

She found solace in the comfort and security enveloping her. Trooper Hunter McCord had a charisma and energy about him that filled the building, making the space seem somehow smaller, yet she didn't mind.

Must be the head trauma.

"Thank you for being here," she said, not at all inclined to step away from the warmth of his embrace. "I'm sorry to be such a burden."

"No apologies necessary." He rubbed her back. "And you're not a burden. This is my job. It's what I do."

Logically she understood he was doing his job. And for some reason a bubble of disappointment floated through her. Odd. There was no reason for her to wish this man wanted to be here because he cared about her. They didn't even know each other. It had to be the upset from the day causing her to be an emotional mess.

So much had transpired in a short space of

time. Had it only been this morning that she'd left to go hiking with Violet?

Worry for her friend crowded her chest. *Please, Lord, let Violet be okay.*

In the distance, the whirling red-and-blue lights of more law enforcement coming meant this night wouldn't be ending anytime soon.

She eased away from the trooper and found his dog was leaning up against her leg as if he too wanted to offer her support.

Hunter smiled. He had a nice smile that crinkled the corners of his blue eyes and made her heart do a little skip. "He likes you."

She tangled her fingers in Juneau's fur. "And I like him."

Ariel had to admit she was thankful for Hunter's and Juneau's presence. If she'd returned home to find the intruder on her own, what would have happened?

She swallowed back the bile rising to burn her throat. A question tore through her mind, making the pounding at her temples increase. "Could the intruder have anything to do with what happened on the mountain?"

Hunter's eyes met hers. "We can't rule anything out."

Exactly what she'd been afraid he'd say.

FOUR

As the Metro patrol cars stopped side by side in the driveway of Ariel's house, Hunter stepped out of the kennel building, followed by Ariel and Juneau. She'd returned his jacket and had put on a barn coat. The dog seemed glued to the woman. Considering her traumatic fall, he was sure the dog sensed she needed comfort, and he respected how well she was holding up after everything she'd been through.

Another vehicle pulled in behind the officers, and there was no mistaking the Alaska K-9 Unit logo on the side of the SUV. His boss, Colonel Lorenzo Gallo, had shown up, as well.

Hunter's surprise gave way to a heavy breath of frustration. He'd let the perp get away. But he'd been more concerned about Ariel and the dogs. He didn't know if whoever had tried to take her dog was working alone or not. Chasing down the suspect would have left Ariel vulnerable and exposed to another attack. And he wasn't going to let anything happen to her on his watch.

This case was proving to be confusing and worrisome. First Ariel was pushed off a cliff and then, later that same night, someone broke into her kennels. Coincidence? Or was she the intended target on the mountain to begin with? But where were her friends? Why kill the tour guide? The questions spun through his mind, turning his brains into cotton candy.

Focusing, he said to Ariel, "I'll be right back." He jogged to Lorenza's side but kept Ariel in his peripheral vision. She stood near the kennel building door with Juneau at her side. "Colonel Gallo?"

"Trooper McCord," Lorenza replied with a sharp nod. Her silver hair peeked out from beneath the edges of her dark blue wool hat. Over her dress suit she wore a calf-length warm coat. "I heard the call come in."

"Any news on the other hikers?"

She shook her head. "Unfortunately, no. Sean and Grace searched the base of the cliff and found nothing." Her gaze zeroed in on Ariel. "This is the victim from the mountain?"

Was no news good news? He wasn't sure in this case. "Yes, ma'am."

"Does what happened tonight have anything to do with what happened on the mountain?"

Hunter blew out a breath. Ariel had asked the same question. "Possibly."

"Two random attacks on one person seem unlikely."

He tended to agree. "Except this wasn't an attack, per se. The suspect attempted to steal her dog."

"Maybe someone followed her up the mountain and tried to get rid of her so they could steal her dog," Lorenza said.

"It's an awful lot of mayhem just to kidnap a dog when they could've easily done the deed while she was out on her hike. As far as I can tell, there's no security system." Something he would have to make sure Ariel remedied.

"Except a pack of dogs," Lorenza said with a glance toward the kennel building, where the sound of dogs howling and vocalizing emanated. Huskies didn't bark but they sure tried to talk.

"Yes, they would definitely sound an alarm," he admitted. "However, Ariel lives alone. A neighbor kid cares for the dogs when she is out. The intruder must have waited until he'd gone home before breaking into the kennels."

"The nearest neighbor is a mile back up the road I drove in on." Her gaze shifted back to the house. "I'd like to meet Miss Potter."

Ariel hung back with her arms wrapped around her middle as if holding herself together.

Juneau remained close, his gaze alert on the police officers climbing out of their cars.

The bandage on her head was a stark reminder of the danger that had come close to ending her life. Something primal tightened in his gut. He never liked to see anyone hurt.

"Ariel," he called to gain her attention. When her gaze swung to him, he waved her over. She moved purposefully to his side.

"Ariel, this is my boss, Colonel Lorenza Gallo. She put together the Alaska K-9 Unit here in Anchorage."

Ariel lifted her chin and stuck out her hand. "It's nice to meet you, Colonel," she said. "I appreciate all that the K-9 Unit has done for me today. Everyone has been so kind and helpful."

Lorenza smiled, her eyes glimmering with approval at the praise of her team. "It's nice to meet you, Miss Potter. You've had quite the day."

Ariel's lips twisted. "That is an understatement. Has there been any word on Violet and the others?"

"No, but we are doing everything we can to find them. Have you given your statement to the police yet?"

Hunter answered, "No, ma'am. We haven't. Everyone arrived at the same time."

"You two need to speak with the officers,"

Lorenza instructed and gestured toward the officers. "Shall we?"

"Yes, ma'am." Hunter put his hand on the small of Ariel's back and guided her forward.

Recognizing Officer Everett Brand from earlier in the day, Hunter introduced his boss and Ariel before explaining the situation. Everett took notes as they talked. It was important that both Hunter and Ariel give their own statements, because perspective was everything. He perceived things through the lens of a cop, while she viewed things through the eyes of a civilian and victim. She might've seen something he hadn't and vice versa.

Two officers fanned out to look for evidence with their flashlights.

"We'll have a crime scene unit come out in the morning when there's daylight," Everett said. "We wouldn't normally pull in CSU for a simple breaking and entering, but since Miss Potter had been so violently assaulted earlier today, we're giving this a more serious response."

"Thank you. I heard an engine start up off in the distance, so the suspect is long gone now," Hunter said. But that didn't mean the intruder hadn't left something behind, like a shoe print or tire print, that might lead them to identifying the would-be thief.

"On the far side of the property line there is

a fire road for the forestry service," Ariel explained.

Lorenza looked at Hunter. "Did you get a good look at the suspect?"

He shook his head. "It was dark. The person was dressed in all black. Average height, slender. It could have been a man, a woman or even a teenager," he replied, wishing he'd been quicker and not let the perpetrator escape.

"We'll have someone check the area out there," Everett said. He focused on Ariel. "Why would someone want to steal one of your dogs?"

Hunter wanted to know the same thing. "Are the dogs chipped?"

"Yes, they are," Ariel answered. "My dogs are worth several thousand dollars apiece. They are all from champion lines and champions themselves."

"That sounds like motive," Everett said.

"But if the thief had succeeded, what were they planning?" Hunter asked. "To claim ownership of the dog? With the chip, passing a stolen dog off as their own would be a risky endeavor."

"Dash, the one the thief tried to take, is slated to sire my next planned litter, which would provide for my first quarter operating expenses. If I'd lost him…" She shivered. "I should check on him and the other dogs."

The sound of tires crunching on the gravel

drew their attention. The veterinarian brought her vehicle to a stop and climbed out.

Dr. Cora Madison hustled over. She was a tall, regal woman with short, dark hair. She wore a thick shearling-lined coat, jeans and snow boots. In one hand she carried a black medical bag. "Hello, everyone."

"Cora, it's good to see you," Lorenza said. The two women shook hands.

"Hey, Doc," Hunter said. "Thank you for coming out."

Cora adjusted her red-framed glasses. "Of course." She moved to Ariel's side and put an arm around her shoulders. "Let's go see our patient."

He noticed the shadows under Ariel's eyes and how her shoulders drooped. She was exhausted and barely functioning. He wanted to alleviate her burden. "I can take you," Hunter said to Cora. "Ariel should go inside and rest."

A flare of surprise widened Ariel's eyes briefly. Then her eyebrows drew together and her gaze narrowed. "I'll rest once I know my dog is okay."

Her affronted tone doused his concern and grated on his nerves. "Ariel—"

"Hunter, let them go." Lorenza's clipped command kept him from saying more. "You and I are not finished."

That sounded ominous. Was she going to bring him to task for letting the suspect get away?

Keeping his frustration in check, he nodded. With a wary look at him, Ariel walked away with Cora. Juneau appeared torn between following Ariel or staying at his partner's side. Hunter gestured for the dog to heel. Juneau moved slowly to his side and sat, but the dog's gaze remained on Ariel. Hunter didn't blame him. He didn't want to let Ariel out of his sight, either, which was strange. She was safe now. There was no reason for him to be so protective.

"I'll go with the ladies," Everett said, taking off after Ariel and Cora.

Hunter couldn't protest, though he wanted to. He wanted to be the one to stick close to Ariel's side. It was his job.

"No need for you to be overbearing. It won't win any points with Miss Potter."

His boss's words jolted through Hunter like a rut in the road. "Excuse me?"

"That young lady seems very independent." Lorenza glanced around and then her gaze landed back on him. "She lives here alone with her pack. I'd imagine she's the one used to giving orders, not taking them."

Hunter's jaw firmed. "Her safety is my responsibility."

There was a slight curve to Lorenza's lips.

"Duly noted." Her expression sobered. "And in that vein, Trooper McCord, I want you to see to Miss Potter's continued safety. Utilize the Metro PD. This woman needs to be guarded 24/7 until we figure out what happened on that mountain."

"Yes, ma'am." Having his boss confirm what he'd already surmised, Hunter's resolve solidified into place. No one would get to Ariel while he was on the case.

When Ariel and Cora entered the kennel building, the dogs all stood. Skye, a beautiful three-year-old agouti Siberian husky, was Sasha's mom. The dog's alternating band of color along each individual hair shaft made her markings unique and sought after as a mama dog. She let out a string of noises that made Ariel wish she could understand the story the dog was telling her.

"I know, girl," Ariel said.

The rest of the dogs watched her, tails wagging. A couple paced, clearly agitated by the chaos.

Empathy for her pack twisted in her chest. Normally when she returned from an outing she'd open each kennel and love on each dog. But at the moment, Dash was the priority.

She led Cora to his kennel at the far end of the

room, grateful to see that Hunter had secured the back door.

"Hey, boy," Ariel greeted him.

Dash rolled from his side, getting his paws beneath him, but that seemed to be as much movement as he could muster. Ariel's heart broke for how close she'd come to losing him. If she and Hunter hadn't returned when they had, Dash would be gone. Stolen. What had the person planned to do with him?

The possibilities made her shudder with dread.

Cora set her black bag on the ground next to the kennel housing Dash before she moved to the sink to wash her hands.

Ariel opened the latch and sat on the floor inside the kennel. Dash lifted his head, his blue eyes nearly black with the pupils so dilated. "I'm here. You're safe now." She stroked his fur. He laid his snout on her knee.

Cora returned to their side and put on latex gloves. "I'll need to get in there."

"Of course." Ariel scooted out so that the vet could take her place inside the kennel.

Cora rubbed her hands over Dash's body. "I'm looking for any obvious signs of injury," she explained. The veterinarian stretched his legs and palpitated his abdomen, took his temperature and other vitals, and checked his eyes, ears, mouth and paws. "Nothing out of the ordinary for him." She combed through his fur, pulling the hair back to view his skin beneath. "Ha. A puncture wound."

"What?" Ariel crowded close to see a small spot crusted with dried blood beneath his fur.

"This puncture is larger than a hypodermic needle would leave behind," Cora said. "I'll take a blood sample, but my best guess would be someone used a tranquilizer dart to subdue him. Something I've seen used on moose and caribou."

Anger at the unknown person churned in Ariel's gut. "Doping him would be the only way anyone he didn't know could get close to him. Is he going to be okay?"

"Yes. How long ago was it that you and Hunter chased off the intruder?"

"Maybe forty minutes or so."

"That's good," Cora said. "Then whatever substance was used is fast acting but wears off fairly quickly. I'll know more once I run his labs." She patted Dash. "He'll be good as new before long."

"Thank God above." Relieved by the prognosis, Ariel backed out of the kennel.

Cora followed her, stripping off her gloves. "I'll call you as soon as I have the results from his blood work and to check on how he's doing. If he shows signs of worsening or refuses to eat or drink, call me and I'll come back out."

"I'd appreciate it." Ariel stood. The world wobbled. She grabbed onto the side of the kennel to let the dizziness pass.

"You should do as Hunter suggested," Cora said with concern lacing her words. "You need to rest. Head injuries are no joke."

"I will." Ariel stood upright and braced her feet apart. "Hunter's words weren't a suggestion but more of a directive."

Cora smiled and pushed her glasses up higher on her straight nose. "He obviously is worried about you."

"He's just doing his job," Ariel said. "He and Juneau were the ones to find me today."

"What happened?"

"Someone pushed me off a cliff." Even saying the words brought a sense of terror slamming into her. "I'd be dead now if a bush hadn't stopped my fall."

Cora drew her in for a hug. "I'm glad God protected you today."

Thankful for the show of kindness and the words of support, Ariel hugged her friend back. "Me, too."

Letting her go, Cora said, "Do you need me to stay with you tonight?"

Nearly brought to tears by the thoughtful offer, Ariel shook her head, then winced at the movement. "No. I'll be fine. You go home to your family." Cora had two school-aged sons and a firefighter husband.

"You shouldn't be alone," Cora said. "I'm worried about you."

"She won't be alone."

Hunter's deep voice made both women turn toward the trooper and his dog striding toward them through the kennel building. Her heart skipped a beat. The pair were so commanding and handsome together. Hunter had put his jacket on, the one he'd let her borrow that had smelled so good. His dark hair was mussed as if he'd run his fingers through the thick strands. A five o'clock shadow darkened his strong jawline, and his eyes appeared more vivid in the overhead fluorescent lights. Juneau also walked with purpose. He obviously wasn't bothered by the animals in their kennels. His focus was on her.

Ariel glanced at her dogs. Though each canine watched with interest, none of them seemed to mind Juneau or Hunter in their space. Interesting. Did the animals have some way of knowing what heroes Juneau and his human partner had been today?

Belatedly, his words sank in, and Ariel wasn't sure she understood exactly what he'd meant. Of course she'd be alone. She didn't have anyone she was comfortable enough with to invite into her house. Plus, wouldn't that put someone else in jeopardy if her attacker decided to come back?

She met his serious blue gaze. "Excuse me?"

"Juneau and I are staying with you," Hunter said, his voice firm. "Tomorrow I'll contact Metro PD to see if they can spare a patrol to keep watch. But for now, you're stuck with us."

Heart rate ticking up, Ariel barely refrained from shaking her head. She didn't want to cause another wave of pain shooting through her brain. "You don't have to do that. I'll be fine."

"It's our job to make sure you're safe," Hunter returned. "So, yes, we do."

Cora touched her elbow, drawing her attention. "Let Hunter protect you. It's the right thing to do."

Stifling a groan, Ariel had to admit the truth in her friend's words. But that didn't mean she had to like the fact that a man would be keeping watch over her. Invading her space. She was very private and used to solitude. The last thing she wanted tonight was to have company.

Taking a calming breath, she decided the smart thing to do was acquiesce. She could handle the intrusion into her life for one night. "I appreciate your offer. I will accept."

A soft smile played at the corners of his mouth, drawing her attention. She liked the shape of his lips and the angular lines of his face. Her gaze drifted to meet his.

Attraction tugged at her, catching her off guard.

He'd saved her life, she reasoned with herself. Of course she'd be drawn to him. And he *was* handsome. There was no denying the obvious. Any woman with a pulse would notice. But none of that mattered.

She wasn't looking for a repeat of her last relationship, nor was she looking for Mr. Right now. Hunter was only temporarily in her life for a specific purpose. To keep her alive.

Because someone had tried to kill her.

The reality of what had happened settled around her like a dark cloak, blocking out all other thought. Her vision tunneled and a buzzing sounded in her ears. Her head pounded behind her eyes.

"Steady there," Hunter's deep voice murmured close to her ear, his hands holding her shoulders, creating hot spots on her biceps.

When had he moved?

Her mouth went dry. "I should sit down."

"Yes, you should," he said. "Let's get you in the house."

"Wait." She struggled to keep her mind from blanking. There were chores that needed to be done. A routine to follow. Things she had to take care of. "I have to let the dogs out one last time."

"I can handle that," Cora said.

"I can't ask you to do my chores," Ariel protested.

"Your dogs know me," Cora replied. "We'll be fine."

"I appreciate the offer, but I want to do it." She needed to reclaim some normalcy, and caring for the dogs would calm her.

A commotion outside the kennel doors had Ariel spinning toward the noise. She yelped with surprise as Hunter tucked her behind him, his hand reaching for his weapon.

"Hey! Stop!" Officer Everett Brand's command jolted through Ariel.

Fear gripped her and she instinctively moved closer to Hunter, gripping the back of his jacket. She reached for Cora to draw her behind Hunter's solid back.

"Okay, okay. I'm looking for Ariel Potter."

Trevor! Ariel had forgotten he was bringing Sasha home. She pushed at Hunter. "It's my neighbor."

"Right." He strode out of the building and returned a moment later with Trevor Nelson and a squirming puppy.

Ariel rushed forward to take Sasha. The puppy

licked her face as she hugged his little body close to her racing heart.

Trevor's eyes were huge in his narrow face. "Ariel, what's going on? Why are the cops here?"

Ariel looked to Hunter, hoping he'd field the questions.

"Miss Potter had a rough day," he said. "Did you notice anyone lurking around the property?"

Trevor shook his head. "No. All was quiet. I left after the evening feeding and exercise time."

Ariel sent a quick prayer of gratitude that the young man hadn't been here when the intruder broke in. "Thank you, Trevor, for caring for the dogs."

She kept a very regimented schedule. Routine was important for the dogs and her. If only she'd stayed with her original plan for the day instead of going up the mountain, maybe none of this would have happened. She wouldn't be hurt, her friends wouldn't be missing and someone wouldn't have tried to steal her dog.

A small voice in her head reminded her she wasn't in control of every aspect of life. She did what she did and now she had to figure out a way forward. "If you'd come by tomorrow I'll pay you."

"Uh, sure." Trevor hesitated as if not sure he should leave. Ariel appreciated the young man's concern.

"It's okay," she assured him. "Everything's fine."

But would everything be fine?

Hunter quietly explained the situation to the young man, telling him to be on alert whenever he came over to help with the dogs.

Hearing the warning sent a shiver of dread down her spine.

Would the assailant come back? And this time succeed in taking Dash and killing her?

FIVE

Hunter appreciated the care and attention Ariel lavished on each dog as she let one canine out at a time into the cordoned-off dog run behind the kennel building. She'd insisted on performing her nightly routine without any help, which had given him the opportunity to feed Juneau from the stash of kibble he kept in his rig while keeping an eye on Ariel in case she needed him. His boss had pegged her correctly. Independent. Used to being the one in control. And Hunter would add stubborn.

Now that all the dogs were back in their respective kennels, Hunter and Juneau escorted Ariel and the puppy to her house. "I still don't understand why you wouldn't ask Trevor to stay and help you," he said as he closed the side door leading into Ariel's kitchen behind him and secured the lock. Once again, he was struck by the coziness of the ranch style home. The kitchen was clean yet looked lived-in with a shining chrome toaster on the granite counter, a fruit basket in the corner filled with apples and pears, and a nice set of cutlery in a wooden block.

Juneau sniffed around the light-colored luxury vinyl flooring, a good choice for a woman with nine dogs because of its scratch-and water-resistant properties.

Ariel placed Sasha inside a medium-size crate in the dining room. The rectangular dining table and four chairs had been pushed up against the wall to allow room for the puppy's crate.

"I just couldn't ask any more of Trevor. He and his mother have already done so much for me."

Hunter leaned against the counter. "What about Cora? She offered to stay and help."

Ariel made a frustrated noise and spun away. She went into the kitchen and grabbed the tea kettle before moving to the sink to fill the pot with water. "The dogs are my responsibility."

He wanted to still her movements, to make her slow down and take a beat. He jammed his hands into the pockets of his jacket instead. "You have a hard time letting others help you."

She set the kettle on the gas stove and lit the flame, then remained with her back to him for a heartbeat.

His observation must have hit a sore spot.

She faced him, her chin jutting out slightly and her light brown eyes sparking. "I learned a long time ago I can only rely on myself. Asking for help is something I do when I have no other option."

That seemed like a hard way to live. What life event had taught her such a harsh lesson? "You could have used the help tonight," he countered. "You sustained a head injury today and should be resting."

"Taking care of the dogs is my pleasure. And routine. I just want some normalcy." She grabbed two cups from the cupboard, shutting the door with more force than necessary. Then she huffed out a breath. "Plus, it seemed safer to send Trevor home." She met his gaze, her expression softening. "I do appreciate your help."

He hadn't done anything other than stand back and watch. The bond between Ariel and the animals was obvious. Each dog was eager to please her while she lavished the same amount of affection on each of them. He'd experienced a strange sort of yearning that had confounded him. What was that about?

"Your dogs are very well behaved."

She smiled, her gaze going to Juneau and back to him. He liked the way her eyes crinkled at the corners when she wasn't worried or upset. "Thank you. I would imagine you train with Juneau as much as I train with my pack."

"Yes, but I'm only working with one dog, not

eight. How do you do that much training and give them each enough attention?" He sometimes suspected he shortchanged Juneau when fulfilling his other duties.

"This is my job. 24/7," she said. "Just as policing is yours. You have to train when not out catching bad guys. Or rescuing people off the side of mountains. These dogs are my only obligation with the exception of the bookkeeping."

The puppy gave a bark and pawed at the door. Ariel opened the crate door and the puppy scampered across the floor, heading straight for Juneau.

Ariel scooped him up before the little guy could reach the bigger dog. Juneau stared at Sasha with his head cocked.

"Juneau wouldn't hurt the puppy," Hunter said.

Ariel smiled at Juneau. "I'm sure you'd be the perfect gentleman. However, this little scamp knows no boundaries. And I would hate for his still-sharp teeth to rip Juneau's ear or cause a wound on his legs or tail. The most likely places Sasha would attack."

Hunter appreciated her concern and her care for Juneau.

The tea kettle whistled. She deposited the puppy into his arms as she moved past him to deal with the boiling water.

He struggled to contain the wiggling ball of

fluff in his hands. Juneau rose from his spot by the side door and moved to sit in front of Hunter, his amber eyes on the puppy.

Sasha's little mouth latched onto Hunter's finger, digging his razor-sharp teeth into Hunter's flesh. "Oh, no you don't." He pried Sasha from his hand and set him on the floor but stepped in the puppy's path to block him from charging Juneau, who rose and dropped his head as if ready to bat away the little dog if need be. "Does he need to go out again?"

"Maybe. Do you mind?"

Shooting her a glance and noting the twinkle in her pretty eyes, he lifted an eyebrow. Apparently, she didn't mind asking him for help taking the puppy out for a break. "Do you have a leash?"

"In the top drawer of the vanity dresser by the front door."

Picking up Sasha in a football hold, Hunter found the bright green leash and harness. He slipped the harness over the small body and latched it. Holding on to the lead, he allowed the puppy to pull him back into the dining room. With Sasha on a leash, Hunter let the scamp sniff Juneau, while the older dog sat and watched, but Hunter tugged Sasha back when the puppy went after Juneau's tail.

"Juneau is very patient," Ariel observed.

"That he is." Hunter couldn't have asked for a

better partner. He trusted Juneau more than he trusted most people.

Ariel opened a cupboard. "Would you like chamomile tea, peppermint tea, spicy tea, black tea, lavender and lemon…"

Half afraid she was going to rattle off every flavor and blend she had in that very packed cupboard, he said, "Okay, hold up. You really like tea."

"I do." She paused with the box of chamomile in her hands. Her delicate eyebrows drew together. "You don't?"

"It's fine. I'll have what you're having."

She nodded and closed the cupboard. "You're a coffee drinker, right?"

"Most days. A little jolt of caffeine proves helpful now and again." He'd started relying on strong black coffee to keep his wits about him while helping his father through the dark days of betrayal by the woman he'd fallen in love with after his retirement from the police force. A decision that had cost his father not only money but his self-respect. A fate Hunter would never allow in his own life. Falling in love was a dangerous endeavor. One he hoped to avoid. He never wanted to be so imprudent as to let his heart rule his head.

"Well, just so you know, there are some teas that have a very high caffeine content."

What kept her up at night that made her seek out caffeine to get through her day? He tucked in his chin. "Good to know."

"But tonight, we'll go with a nice herbal blend. I'll let the teas steep while you let the dogs out." She put a tea bag in each cup.

He chuckled at her pointed instructions. "All right, fellas, you heard the lady, outside." He unlocked and opened the side door. Juneau waited for Hunter to release him before he trotted through the open doorway into the glow of the outside lights.

Hunter and the puppy followed. The frigid April air stung Hunter's lungs. He searched the area for signs of any threats while the puppy sniffed the grass. Juneau disappeared around the corner of the house and came back a few minutes later.

Satisfied that all was well on the property, with no dogs howling to signal an intruder, he urged the puppy back into the house. Juneau slipped inside and lay down beside Sasha's crate as if he knew that was where the puppy was headed.

After removing the harness from the puppy, Hunter tucked him inside the crate and set the latch on the door. Sasha lay down with his black nose sticking through the wire holes, nearly touching Juneau.

Hunter returned to the kitchen, where Ariel

handed him a cup of chamomile tea. The fragrant scent of the chamomile flower wafted up with the steam rising from the mug. He wrapped his hands around the ceramic and let the heat seep into his cold fingers.

He followed Ariel into the living room. She sat on an overstuffed wingback chair, tucking her feet up beneath her. He took a position on the couch facing the large picture window that looked out over the drive. Juneau left the sleeping puppy to lie down in front of Ariel's chair.

She glanced down at him. "Do you train him to do that with all your rescue victims?"

"Only the pretty ones," he quipped, then inwardly cringed. Where did that come from?

Her eyes widened and then lowered to look into her tea as if the world's secrets could be found in the soothing depths of her mug.

Great, she probably believed he was flirting with her. He was usually much better at keeping his thoughts from escaping. Hoping to alleviate the sudden tension between them, he said, "Tell me more about your business?"

Lifting her gaze, she said, "My dad was a champion musher until he had an accident that left him with a bum knee. But he loved the sport so much that he decided to start breeding dogs and training them for other mushers."

"And he taught you?"

"Yes, I kind of learned alongside him," she replied. "We had dogs traveling with us for as far back as I can remember. My mother and I would go with my father on the race circuit around the US and Europe."

"Did he compete in the Iditarod?"

"He did, and usually placed in the top fifty."

"That must have been a very interesting childhood," he remarked.

"It was lonely," she admitted. "Just me and my parents."

Empathy twisted in his chest. "I don't have siblings, either."

"Being an only child does lend itself to loneliness, doesn't it?"

As did losing his mother at a young age. A subject he didn't want to talk about. "So, you traveled with your parents during the racing season. I assume you went to school the rest of the time?" He wasn't sure of the time frame for the racing season beyond the famed Iditarod, which started in Anchorage at the beginning of March and ended fifteen days later in Nome.

She shifted in the chair and leaned her head back and then winced, sitting straight up. "No, my mother homeschooled me."

Which meant she hadn't had school friends. "Were there other children on the race circuit?"

"Some. But there wasn't ever time to form any

real attachments." She shrugged. "We traveled to places that some people only dream about. The excitement of race day was always something I looked forward to and, truth be told, still do."

"Hard to show off champion dogs without putting them to the test," he said.

"Exactly. Plus the purse money helps with my operating expenses."

"You do it all. Impressive."

"Training the dogs is my passion." She made a face, her nose scrunching up in an adorable way that had his gut clenching. "When I was old enough for high school, my parents decided it was time for me to enter the public school system. They dropped me off with my grandparents here in Anchorage."

"Difficult adjustment, I would imagine." He remembered his high school days. All the jockeying for popularity. The dramas between classmates. Everything seemed so much more important and life-altering until stepping onto a college campus.

"I got through it. College was better. That's where I met Violet." Ariel's gaze dropped to her tea. "I can't believe she hasn't been found yet." She lifted her gaze, her eyes filled with worry. "Do you think she's okay?"

He wished he could reassure her but there was

no reassurance he could formulate. He answered honestly, "I pray so."

"I do, too."

"Tell me more about Violet." Maybe something Ariel knew about her friend might help them understand where she was or what had happened to her and the other two hikers.

"Violet came from wealth, but she doesn't flaunt it. She's kind and generous. Big-hearted. She recently become a Christian and dedicated her life to the Lord. And then she found out that she was pregnant with Lance's baby…"

"How did Lance feel about the baby? Is that why they were getting married?"

Ariel made a face. "Lance didn't know. She planned to tell him, but I don't know if she worked up the nerve to do it."

Hunter's mind turned this information over in his head. "Could she and Lance have eloped?"

Ariel perked up. "Now that's an idea." She frowned, her shoulders slumping. "But it doesn't explain who killed the tour guide or why somebody would push me off the edge of a cliff. And where's Jared?"

"Good questions." This case was certainly a mystery. He noticed her stifling a yawn and glanced at his watch. It was well after midnight. "I should let you get some sleep."

He took their mugs to the sink and rinsed them

out. When he returned to the living room, she had collected a blanket and pillow for the couch.

"Would Juneau like a pillow, too?" she asked.

"He'll be fine. Most likely he'll plant himself by the front door." Hunter checked that all the window and door locks were secure.

Ariel retrieved Sasha from his crate and snuggled him to her chest. "Thank you, Hunter, for everything," she murmured and headed down the darkened hallway to the room at the end.

When he heard the soft snick of the door closing, he dimmed the lights and stretched out on the couch. His utility belt dug into his hip. He debated taking it off, then decided it was best to leave it in place. Juneau flopped down on the entryway tile by the front door.

Hunter closed his eyes but kept seeing Ariel balanced precariously on the bush jutting out from the side of the mountain. He prayed until he drifted off to a light sleep.

His phone vibrating in his front shirt pocket brought him fully awake. He glanced at his watch. Three in the morning.

"McCord," he rasped into the phone.

"Hey, it's Gabe." Fellow Trooper Gabriel Runyon's voice filled the line. "Dispatch received a call from our missing groom. Lance Wells and Jared Dennis used a satellite phone to report that they were injured and holed up in a cabin in Chugach State Park."

"Is Violet James with them?"

"They didn't say. The colonel asked me to mobilize a search team. She wants you with us."

Hunter sat up and wiped a hand over his jaw, the rough whiskers scratching his palm. He couldn't leave Ariel unguarded. "I'll meet you at the state park entrance as soon as I can. I need to arrange for Metro PD to send over a patrol officer."

"Copy that," Gabriel said.

Hunter hung up, dialed the precinct and asked for Officer Everett Brand. A few moments later dispatch connected him to the officer.

"Brand here."

"Everett, this is Hunter from the Alaska K-9 Unit. I'm hoping you can help me out. I'm at Miss Potter's, but I've been called away. I need you to come stand guard until I can return. She'll be more comfortable with someone she's already familiar with."

"I'm on my way. I'll arrange for someone to take over in the morning if you're not available by then."

"I'd appreciate that." Hunter hung up. He didn't relish waking Ariel up to tell her what was happening, but he knew if he left without saying anything she would be upset. Besides, she deserved to know that Lance made contact.

He walked down the dark hall and softly knocked on her bedroom door. It opened almost immediately. The soft glow of her bedside lamp backlit her as she stood in the doorway.

"I heard voices," she said.

"It was me on the phone. Lance Wells sent out an SOS message saying he and Jared need rescuing. Juneau and I need to go help in the search."

"Violet?"

"No word yet."

She made a distressed noise. "Where could she be?"

He hated seeing the anxiousness in Ariel's expression. "She might be with them. Don't lose hope."

Ariel took a shuddering breath. "I'm trying not to."

She pushed past him and headed for the living room. "You should go. I'll be fine here."

"Not quite so fast. Officer Brand is coming to provide you protection."

Her lips pursed. "Okay. I appreciate all you're doing for me. For Violet and the guys. Please bring them back, Hunter."

He knew better than to make a promise he had no guarantee of keeping. "I will do my best."

* * *

Ariel cuddled Sasha to her chest and stared out the front window as Hunter's taillights disappeared down the drive. The darkness enveloped his vehicle, leaving her somehow bereft of his and Juneau's presence.

Officer Brand sat in his car, parked near the front porch. He shouldn't be out in the cold like that, but he refused to come inside, stating he was used to long overnight stakeouts.

Needing something to do, she went to the kitchen and made a thermos full of hot cocoa. Then she put on her barn boots and jacket, and she and Sasha went out to deliver the thermos to the policeman.

Officer Brand rolled down his passenger side window. "Miss Potter?"

"Hot cocoa." She handed him the thermos. "It's the least I can do."

"Thank you. That's very thoughtful of you."

"I'll be sleeping in the kennel room with the dogs," she told him. "The house is too quiet." Not usually a problem for her. But she had to admit she was a little freaked out and nervous about this whole ordeal. She wanted the comfort of her canine companions. "I appreciate you being out here."

"Doing my job, ma'am."

A refrain she'd heard already once today from

Hunter. Were all law enforcement types so dedicated to their jobs? What else was Hunter dedicated to? Did he have a wife waiting for him at home? Guilt pricked her conscience. Had she kept him away from his family? And now here was this nice officer also sacrificing his time to protect her.

All because someone had tried to kill her.

With a shiver of unease, she went back inside. There was no way she'd fall asleep. Her insides were twisted in knots of worry for her friend. Grabbing the blanket and pillow from the couch, she stopped at the entryway closet for the baseball bat she kept there. Then she and Sasha headed out to the kennel room.

The dogs perked up as she entered. She checked on each dog before settling down next to Dash's kennel. She made herself a little nest and lay on her side in a position that didn't bother her wounded head. The pillow smelled like Hunter, spicy and masculine. Sasha turned circles in front of her before settling down and scooting up next to her belly. Dash put his paw through the wire grating, and she held on to him. As she worked to calm her racing thoughts, she whispered, "Please, Lord, bring Hunter and Violet back to me."

SIX

Once again traversing the fresh-snow-covered trail leading up to Flattop Mountain, Hunter's mind was half attentive to where the search party was headed. The other half of his brain was focused back at Ariel's house.

Was she safe?

He pushed the question aside. Of course she was. Officer Brand would see to her safety.

Yet Hunter couldn't deny that trusting others to do their jobs the way he wanted the job done didn't come easy.

One of his many flaws, as his father kept telling him.

He expected too much of people.

But no more than he expected from himself.

Was she scared?

Well, duh. Someone tried to kill Ariel. He'd hated seeing the fear in her eyes when he'd left her standing in the doorway of her home, holding the puppy, looking so sweet and vulnerable.

He didn't understand why she got to him in such a visceral way.

He shook his head. Best to get his brain in gear and focus on the task at hand.

The early morning air clung to his breath every time he exhaled. Tension twisted his gut into knots. They didn't know what they were going to find or what they would have to deal with once they reached the coordinates for the cabin where the groom and the best man were holed up.

Gabriel and Bear led the way, paused and pointed off to the right side of the mountain, away from the place where they had found Ariel and the tour guide. "That way."

"How did they double back down the mountain and go this direction without anyone seeing them?" Hunter asked. Was this some sort of ruse to draw them away from Ariel? The muscles in his shoulders bunched as the overwhelming need to return to her gripped him, making him misstep, nearly taking a header into the snow. Juneau glanced over his shoulder at him, his eyes bright in the dawning light.

"Maybe they went over the top of the mountain and down the other side," Maya said. "I saw no indications of them doubling back when we were up there earlier yesterday."

"That makes sense," Gabriel agreed.

"There's no way we will get an ambulance back here," Maya observed.

Hunter's flashlight swept over the path ahead of them. The rough terrain, especially with the new fall of snow, was perfect for the snow machines. "I'll call EMS and request snowmobiles."

"It's a good idea." There was a hint of mocking amusement in Gabriel's tone, his kind way of reminding Hunter who was leading the search party.

Hunter let out a breath. He liked to be in control. Another of his many flaws. One he shared with Ariel. He shrugged. "Sorry. After you."

Gabriel clapped him on the back as he stepped past him and led Bear into the snow.

Hunter and Juneau followed, while Hunter made the call. The snow was deep and required effort to plow through, but the dogs were agile and easily navigated the drifts, occasionally stopping to shake, sending snow flying.

As the dark gave way to twilight, the outline of the cabin tucked beneath a grove of spruce and hemlock trees became visible. They fanned out and approached the A-frame structure with caution. Hunter and Juneau headed to the left, Maya to the right, and Gabriel straight to the front door.

Hunter edged around the side of the cabin and peeked inside through a chest-high, rectangular window. Dirt and snow covered the glass pane.

Through the streaks of dirt, he could make out someone lying on a cot. But Hunter didn't see anyone else. Gabriel's loud knock on the front door broke the silence.

"Alaska K-9 Unit. Open up."

The creak of the door opening sent a chill over Hunter. Light filtered in through the open doorway, illuminating the person on the bed. He wasn't sure, but it looked to be Jared Dennis.

Hunter and Juneau circled the building, meeting up with Maya and Sarge in the front. Gabriel and Bear had stepped inside the cabin. Hunter, Juneau, Maya and Sarge crowded inside behind Gabriel and Bear, shutting the door to keep the cold out.

Lance Wells, holding a rag to his head, shuffled backward. He was tall with short, dark blond hair, and his green eyes watched them warily. He was dressed in black snow pants, marred with dirt, and a dark jacket that had a rip down the side. He gave his head a shake, winced, then said, "I'm so glad to see you."

Jared Dennis lay stretched out on the cot with what looked like a bloodied T-shirt wrapped about the upper biceps of his right arm. His brown hair had leaves sticking out like ornaments on a tree.

Lance sat down on the cot and jostled his friend. "Jared, wake up. Help is here."

The man came to with a moan, his eyelids fluttering open. He licked his lips. "Water?"

Maya hustled forward with a small bottle of water from her pack. She helped the man drink some of the liquid, then handed Lance another small bottle of water.

Lance downed the contents in a few gulps. He wiped his mouth with the back of his hand. "Thank you."

Hunter took out a notepad from his jacket pocket and a pen. Knowing how worried Ariel was for her friend, he asked, "Where's Violet James?"

"She's not here," Lance said. "That woman is crazy."

Hunter's chest tightened.

Gabriel stepped forward. "Tell us what happened and how you came to be here."

Lance put his hands on his knees and bent forward as if he was going be sick. He took a few deep breaths before he sat back up. "It was Violet. She did this to us. She shot Jared."

"Where did she get the gun?" Hunter demanded.

"How should I know!" Lance raised his voice. "She conked me on the head. I lost consciousness. Jared tried to wrestle the gun from her, and she shot him."

Maya moved forward to evaluate the man's injury. "It's a through and through. Doesn't look like it hit the bone." She glanced at Lance. "You did a good job of stopping the blood flow."

When she moved back, Jared rolled to prop himself up on his uninjured arm. "Violet shot the tour guide and she pushed her friend over the side of the cliff."

"Poor Ariel." Lance hung his head. "To be killed by your best friend."

Only she wasn't dead as they assumed.

"We found the tour guide, Cal Brooks," Gabriel said.

"Please, you have to find Ariel's body. She deserves a good memorial." Lance's eyes teared up.

"We have found Ariel," Hunter added, unwilling to reveal more just yet. The need to protect her burned bright within him. "Why would Violet shoot the tour guide and push Ariel over the cliff?"

Lance scrubbed a hand over his face. "Violet was having an affair with that man."

Tucking in his chin, Hunter stared. Really? Did Ariel know this? Had she kept that information from him? Hunter jotted down what Lance had said.

"With Cal Brooks?" Maya said. "How do you know they were having an affair?"

"He told me." Lance's wild-eyed gaze bounced between Hunter, Gabriel and Maya. "That's why she shot him. In cold blood. Just pulled out a gun and shot him."

"You saw her do this?" Gabriel questioned.

"Yes," Lance answered as he jumped to his feet.

Hunter put his hand on his weapon. All three dogs emitted a low growl.

Eyeing the dogs with concern, Lance said, "She took our phones and marched us here. She knocked me out and left us to die."

Hunter had trouble wrapping his mind around this information. This didn't sound anything like the woman whom Ariel had described. But then again, he should know how easily fooled some people could be. His father, a seasoned cop, had been duped by Celeste. Hunter would never make the same mistake. Maybe Ariel was keeping secrets. If so, Hunter would ferret them out just as he had with Celeste.

However, someone had pushed Ariel over the cliff and tried to steal her dog. Those were the facts that couldn't be denied. And his gut said Ariel was innocent. Ugh. His mind was going in circles. He needed to focus.

Had Violet suffered a psychotic break? Hunter made a note to have Katie check with the James family about the missing woman's medical history.

"How were you able to call for help?" Maya asked.

Lance pointed to the card table in the corner of the cabin. "We found that satellite phone here." He sucked in air, his agitation growing. "Violet has lost it. You have to find her before she hurts more people."

"I'll call this in," Maya said, and she and Sarge stepped out of the cabin.

Gabriel focused his gaze on Hunter. "We'll take a look around outside. You okay here with them?"

"Affirmative." He wanted a few aspects of the men's story clarified. As soon as Gabriel and Bear exited, he stared at the two men. "Walk me through the day. Start at the beginning."

Lance sat back down as if his legs couldn't hold him any longer. "It was supposed to be a wonderful, prewedding adventure. Violet loves adventures. I thought she'd enjoy going on an off-the-beaten-path hike." He pinched the bridge of his nose. "Next thing I know, Cal's saying, *I'm telling him.* She hissed at him to be quiet. Then Cal said they were having an affair and she wasn't going to marry me." His voice broke on the last word.

Hunter took notes, his mind going back to what Ariel had said about Violet being pregnant. Was that a lie? Or was the bride-to-be actually pregnant, but the identity of the father was in doubt? He decided to keep that information to himself until he determined exactly what the truth was.

"Then she pulled a gun from her jacket pocket and she—" Lance covered his face with his hands.

"She shot the tour guide point-blank in the chest," Jared said. "There was no remorse, no nothing in her eyes. She has the coldest blue eyes."

"We ran." Lance dropped his hands back to his knees. "She shot at us. When she missed she turned and ran for Ariel."

Hunter cocked his head. "You saw her push Ariel over the cliff?"

Jared nodded. "I did. When Violet took off, Lance went to help Cal to see if he was alive. And I followed Violet, intending to help Ariel, but I was too late. She shoved the poor girl off the cliff. I ran back and got Lance and we started running."

"And Violet came after you?" Hunter tried to envision how this played out.

"Yes, she did." Lance's voice shook. "She caught up to us. Took our phones and marched us here. Once we got inside she shot Jared but it was her last bullet, so she knocked me over the head with the butt of her gun. She left us here to die. No heat, no water, no food. Nothing. If we hadn't found that satellite phone—" His breathing came in big gulping gasps.

"Right," Hunter said. "If you hadn't found the satellite phone, we wouldn't have been able to find you. But how did you know where you were?"

"There's a brochure," Jared replied. "This is a public-use cabin. Apparently, nobody reserved it for this weekend."

"And when I came to, I used my T-shirt to dress Jared's wound," Lance said.

Was what they were saying true? If so, this would devastate Ariel. Hunter didn't have a reason to suspect they were lying, which meant they had an armed and dangerous woman on the loose.

Where had Violet gone?

The sound of snowmobile engines coming closer alerted Hunter of EMS's arrival. "You two stay put," he said and walked out the cabin door with Juneau at his heels. He tucked his notebook into his pocket. Something about this whole situation had his hackles up, yet he had no reason to doubt the two men. Why would they make up such an elaborate scenario?

Gabriel and Bear joined Hunter and Juneau on the front porch.

The headlights from the snowmobiles stopping ten feet away mixed with the rising sun illuminated the shiny object dangling from Gabriel's fingers. "What's that?"

"I assume our suspect's bracelet," Gabriel said. "Look at the initials on the charm. VJ."

Violet James's bracelet. Proof that she'd been in the area? Hunter's stomach clenched. Was she close by? His gaze scanned the shadowed trees surrounding the cabin. "While you get these guys loaded onto the snowmobiles, Juneau and I are going to search the area." He knew if there was even a trace of Violet's scent left on the piece of jewelry, Juneau would detect it. "Let him sniff the bracelet."

Gabriel lowered the charm bracelet to Juneau's nose.

"Find," Hunter said to the dog.

Juneau lifted his nose to the air and then down to the ground, then back to the air before looping away from the cabin. Hunter went after him, praying he found Violet and she would come peacefully. For Ariel's sake.

Morning turned into afternoon and still no word from Hunter. Ariel had gone about her daily chores, very aware of the police car sitting on the front drive. Officer Brand had been relieved by a younger officer named Bruce Grayson. Throughout the course of the day, Ariel had checked on the officer, offering him hot coffee and use of the facilities.

Dash was back to his old self, though Ariel noticed he was more protective of her and stuck close by while the other dogs were released into the fenced yard for some much-needed recreational time with the plethora of toys that she kept for them.

She'd removed the bandage from her head hours ago and barely noticed any residual pain where she'd sustained a laceration on the back of her scalp.

After putting the dogs through their exercises and training for the day, Ariel returned them to their kennels with their evening meal.

Taking the puppy with her inside the house, she fed Sasha and put him in his crate so she could prepare her own dinner. Anxiety twisted in her chest. Why hadn't Hunter called? There had to be a reason. Maybe he'd found Violet, Lance and Jared. Worry chomped through her like a hungry beast as awful scenarios played through her mind. Were they all dead? Killed by a bullet or a fall?

"This is ridiculous," she groused aloud, eliciting a howl from Sasha as if in agreement.

With a quick twist of the knob, she turned off the burner on the stove that had been heating her spaghetti sauce and grabbed her phone. She was going to call the K-9 Unit and demand answers.

Unfortunately, the dispatch person who answered said there was no new information they could give her but promised to have Hunter call her soon as he checked in. Why hadn't he touched base? What was happening on the mountain? Was he hurt?

A different kind of concern arched through her, making her shiver with dread.

Please, Lord, no more tragedies.

She ate only a small portion of her dinner because her stomach was too tied in knots for very much food. Needing something to do, she took a plate out to the young officer.

"That's mighty nice of you, ma'am," Officer Grayson said.

"Are you sure you wouldn't rather come inside?" she asked. "You'd be so much warmer."

"Oh, no, ma'am. I'm fine here. I'm actually getting a lot of my computer work done." He flashed her a grin.

As grateful as she was that all was quiet and he was able to work, she couldn't shake the trepidation making her skin crawl. Her gaze roamed over the forested land rimming her property. Was someone out there watching? Waiting to strike?

What enemy had she made who was determined to hurt her?

Wrapping her arms over her middle she went back inside and dug into her own bookkeeping.

As darkness fell, casting shadows over her work, the frantic howls of her pack filled the air, causing the fine hairs at her nape to quiver with alarm.

The dogs sounded like they had the night before when an intruder tried to steal Dash.

Panicked, she raced out the door, her gaze going to the cruiser. She could see the deputy inside. But the dome light was off and all she could make out was his silhouette. Ariel debated going out to get him versus checking on her dogs. She knew what Hunter would want her to do—seek out the safety of the officer.

So she went with her gut.

As she ran for the cruiser, the sound of a rush of footsteps behind her chilled her bones. A sense of déjà vu struck her like lightning, her whole body vibrating with terror.

She spun to face the oncoming threat just as hands grabbed her around her neck and squeezed. A blur of dark clothing registered in her brain as she fought with every ounce of strength she possessed. Using her elbows and her heels, she kicked and screamed, eliciting a high-pitched yelp from her attacker. But the hands gripping her were strong, cutting off her air supply.

Bright lights swung across the driveway, stinging her eyes. Abruptly she was released. She crumpled to the ground in a heap.

SEVEN

Slamming the gear shift into Park, Hunter jumped from his vehicle while calling dispatch for EMS. His heart hammered in his chest. The image of someone with their hands wrapped around Ariel's throat etched into his mind in the brief flash of the headlights made fear, stark and cold, run through his veins. Using his key fob, he released the side door of the vehicle, allowing Juneau to leap out of the SUV. Then Hunter ran to where Ariel lay unmoving on the ground while a slim figure dressed in a dark hoodie sprinted away, disappearing into the darkness. Juneau chased the assailant, but Hunter whistled to bring the dog back. He wouldn't risk Juneau getting hurt.

Gently, Hunter rolled Ariel to her back and cradled her head to keep the pressure off the head wound she'd received when she'd fallen off the cliff. "Ariel. Can you hear me?"

Juneau licked her face and nudged her with his nose.

He checked for a pulse, fully prepared to begin lifesaving measures. Her heart beat strong beneath his fingertips, easing the constriction in his chest a fraction. He leaned close, putting his ear near her mouth and nose. Her breath fanned over his face.

"Hunter?"

He turned to look at her face and found her big brown eyes watching him. He let out a silent prayer of thanksgiving that he'd heeded the urge to check on her. "You're safe. I've got you."

"There was a—" She coughed, her whole body shaking with the effort to expel air through what was no doubt a painful throat.

"Shh. Don't try to talk. An ambulance is coming," Hunter said. "I saw your attacker run away." He wanted badly to go after the perpetrator, but Ariel's safety was his first priority.

"A woman," she managed to say, her voice coming out raspy.

Acid burned in Hunter's stomach. *Violet.* Had she returned to finish what she'd started on the mountain? Was Violet the one who'd tried to steal Dash last night? Why? What motive had sent Ariel's best friend on a killing rampage?

His heart wrenched with the anticipation of

having to tell Ariel what Lance and Jared had shared about Violet's horrific actions.

She gripped his arm and pulled herself to a seated position. "The officer."

Hunter's gaze whipped around to the cruiser parked off to the side of the entrance. When Hunter had turned into the drive and had seen Ariel being attacked, all of his attention had centered on getting to her and keeping her alive. Now he realized something was definitely wrong. Where was the officer? Had Violet gotten to him, too?

Hunter's chest tightened. He should've been here to protect Ariel. "Can you stand?"

She nodded and grasped his hand. He helped her to her feet and put an arm around her waist. She leaned into him. The flowery scent of her shampoo clinging to her hair wrapped around him, a heady aroma that he would not likely forget. Together, with Juneau sticking close to her side, they approached the Metro police cruiser. The officer sat unmoving in the driver's seat. The interior of the car was too dark to ascertain if the man was injured.

Afraid of what they would find inside, Hunter leaned Ariel against the front bumper. "Stay put," he said. "Let me check on him."

With dread knotting his gut, Hunter approached the driver side window. It was down.

The young officer sat slumped, his chin to his chest. The seat belt was the only thing keeping the officer upright. Hunter reached through the open window and pressed two fingers against the man's neck. He was alive. Hunter breathed out a relieved breath. But what had happened to him?

A siren growing closer heralded the arrival of the ambulance.

"Is the officer okay?" Ariel said, her voice hoarse.

Hunter went to her side. "He's alive."

He couldn't comment as to whether he was okay or not. Until they knew what had knocked him out, there was no guarantee that the young officer would survive this ordeal.

Hunter waved the ambulance forward and had them park near the cruiser. The two EMS personnel jumped out.

"We have an attempted strangulation victim," Hunter told the pair and gestured to Ariel.

One paramedic tended to Ariel, checking her airway and her heart rate, while the other checked on the unconscious officer.

"We need to get this man to the hospital," the paramedic said. "I don't see a wound. I'd hazard a guess he's been drugged."

Like Dash had been. Hunter was confident the doctors would find the same substance in the officer as the vet found in Dash. He turned to the other paramedic and Ariel. "How is she?"

"She should be seen at the hospital to assess damage to the vocal chords and have a CT angiogram to check if there's injury to the vessels in the neck."

Ariel made a face and shook her head. "I don't want to go back to the hospital."

"I don't like hospitals, either, but you need medical attention," Hunter said, then turned to both paramedics. "I'll take her. You take the officer. We'll follow."

Ariel tugged at Hunter's sleeve. "The dogs."

"I'll arrange for another guard to come out and watch over them."

"Trevor," Ariel said. "Call him, too."

"Where's your phone?"

She pointed to the house.

Once again tucking her close to his side and holding her about the waist, he gave the medics room to move the officer onto a gurney and put him into the back bay of the ambulance. Then Hunter helped Ariel into the house, where she directed him to her cell phone sitting on a charger. Juneau sniffed around the floor as she scrolled through her contacts, then handed Hunter the device.

He hit the send button.

Trevor answered on the third ring. "Hello?"

"Trevor, this is Trooper McCord with the Alaska K-9 Unit. We met yesterday."

"Yeah?" There was no mistaking the wariness in the younger man's tone.

"I'm at Miss Potter's place and she needs your help. I'm taking her to the hospital. Would you be willing to come and stay with the dogs?"

"Whoa. Dude, what happened? What's going on?"

Hunter figured the boy needed to know enough to be prepared. "Like I explained before, somebody has been targeting Miss Potter. She would appreciate having someone here the dogs know."

"That's messed up," the kid said. "I'll be right over."

Hunter then called Metro PD, explained to dispatch the situation and requested another officer to come to Ariel's property.

He hung up the phone and turned to Ariel. She sat on a dining room chair, holding her head in her hands. Juneau was perched at her feet, his amber eyes watching her.

Hunter knelt down before her. "You doing okay? Do you need to throw up?"

She shook her head and lifted her gaze to meet his. "Water."

He filled a mug and brought it to her. She took the cup and drank a few sips. After a moment she handed it back to him. She swallowed several times and cleared her throat.

"Thanks. I'm getting better already," she said, though the raspy tone of her voice hadn't lessened. "It hurts less. I don't need to go to the hospital."

"Right." He held out his hand. "Let's go."

She clutched his hand but didn't move. "You came in the nick of time. God sent you."

Hunter wasn't sure if God had prompted him to return to her place after leaving headquarters or not, but he was grateful he'd arrived in time. He'd finished up his paperwork and had seen the message that she'd called. If God was at work here, Hunter was thankful.

"Tell me about Violet," she urged. "What did you find on the mountain today?"

Not ready to delve into Lance and Jared's accusation, he said, "Let's get you to the hospital and checked out before we deal with that." He tugged her to her feet.

She wobbled, then steadied herself by flexing her knees and holding on to him. "No, I have to know."

He rubbed her hands between his, holding her gaze. As much as he knew the news would hurt her, he had to tell her at some point and if she insisted on hearing it now, then he would accommodate her. "We found Lance and Jared. They claim that Violet shot Cal Brooks."

"What?" She winced and yanked her hands from his to clutch her throat. "No."

"This is why I didn't want to tell you yet. You need to heal before you face all of this."

She lowered her hands and tilted her head slightly to keep eye contact. "I want all of it. Now. I'm not—" She swallowed and turned away to grab the mug. After taking a few sips, she set the cup back down, then faced him again. "I am not some fragile flower that can't handle the truth," she said between clenched teeth. "Tell me everything."

"Lance claims that Violet was having an affair with Cal Brooks and Cal wanted to come clean about it."

Ariel stepped back and shook her head. "That's not true."

Knowing his next words were going to cause her anguish, Hunter closed the distance between them, ready to steady her if needed. "Lance and Jared claim that Violet pushed you over the side of the cliff."

For a prolonged heartbeat, she stared with a stunned expression that had him fighting the urge to draw her to his chest and hold her. Ariel's sweet face registered shock, then denial as her eyes darkened, and she pushed past him to place her hands on the kitchen counter. Her shoulders sagged as she gasped for breath. Then she seemed to gather her composure. She straightened, lifting her chin, and turned to face him. "It's not true. None of it. They're liars."

He grimaced. "But what do they hope to gain by lying?"

"I don't know, but I intend to find out. I want to see them."

He could only imagine what it was costing her, both physically and emotionally, to be so strong. "We need to go to the hospital."

A stubborn light entered her eyes. "Lance and Jared first."

"Like I said, we're going to the hospital. That's where they are."

Her eyebrows dipped together. "Why didn't you say that to begin with? Let's go." She grabbed her wallet and keys off the sideboard next to where she had her phone charging. Then she stopped. Panic etched into her features. "Where's Sasha? I didn't put him in his crate."

Hunter grabbed her by the biceps as she swayed. "We'll find him. You sit down before you pass out." He helped her to the dining chair. "Could he be outside?"

She frowned. "I don't know."

She started to rise, but he held up a hand. "I've got this."

Deciding to start the search indoors, he called out, "Sasha!"

Hunter walked through the living room and down the hallway with Juneau at his heels. There was only one door opened. He and Juneau entered Ariel's inner sanctuary. The room was a burst of color with a bright flowered bedspread and a variety of pink, orange and yellow throw pillows piled high on the bed. A deep burgundy comfy chair in the corner near a bookshelf provided an inviting space to sit and read. Hunter could imagine Ariel sitting there at the end of the day with a book and a cup of tea.

His gaze zeroed in on the puppy. Sasha lay curled up on a fluffy round dog bed wedged between the side of Ariel's bed and the wall. The puppy lifted his head and gave a little yelp of joy as he bounded out of the bed and across the floor, jumping on Juneau. Juneau backed up a step, dropped his head and nudged the puppy backward. Sasha plopped onto his hindquarters.

"You little scamp." Hunter scooped the puppy up and cradled him close to his chest. "Your mom is going be very glad to know that you are okay."

When they returned to the dining room, Ariel had her hands folded on her lap and her head bowed.

Hunter stopped. The sight of her praying lit a

fire in his heart. She'd suffered so many traumas in a short amount of time and yet she still believed, still looked to God for help and answers. She was an amazing woman. And he had better figure out a way to keep her from invading his heart. He wasn't interested in any type of long-term commitment beyond this assignment.

Aware of Hunter's gaze, Ariel finished her prayer, thanking God for saving her life yet again. And she also thanked Him for bringing Hunter and Juneau to the rescue.

She opened her eyes and her heart stalled in her chest as her gaze landed on the big, handsome state trooper tenderly holding the little Alaskan husky in his arms, his beautiful K-9 partner at his side. The itch to photograph the man and dogs dug at her like a thorn. If only her camera hadn't been smashed in the fall.

Why wasn't she more alarmed at having Hunter in her space? Unaccountably, there was something comfortable about being with the man. He'd saved her life multiple times. It didn't mean anything beyond he was good at his job and God was watching out for her. She couldn't put any more importance on the emotions bouncing around inside her, not if she wanted to stay safe from heartache. Which she did. She'd learned long ago not to allow herself to rely on others for her happiness. It never worked out. Not with her parents. Not with Jason.

She rose and reached for Sasha.

"He was sleeping in his bed," Hunter said as he handed over the puppy.

As she nuzzled Sasha, his soft fur tickling her skin and his rough tongue scraping across her cheek with kisses, relief that he hadn't escaped out the door or gotten into anything harmful made her limbs quiver. The adrenaline ebbing from her body was making the pain in her throat and head throb.

"As soon as Trevor gets here as well as the other officer, we can go," Ariel said, not at all looking forward to what was to come. She'd need every ounce of strength to confront Lance and Jared. Why were they telling such vicious lies about Violet? "But I'd like to see the dogs now. Let them know I'm okay."

Hunter nodded and they walked out to the kennel room. She didn't believe a word of what Lance and Jared claimed. Violet would not have shot anyone. And she definitely would not have pushed Ariel over the cliff. They had been friends far too long and had gone through too many dramas and heartbreaks and joyous occasions together. There was just no way. And there was nothing anyone was going to be able to say to make her believe that Violet had that kind of malice in her.

Inside the kennel room, she greeted each dog with a quick pat to let the pack know she was unharmed. And once again her dogs didn't seem to mind Juneau or Hunter. Which was odd considering every dog was an alpha in their own right.

A knock on the kennel building door jolted through her. Hunter looked at her and put up his hand, stopping her from going to the door.

She gestured for him to answer the knock, her stomach knotting with nerves. But she rationalized that a killer wouldn't announce their presence, would they?

A moment later, Hunter ushered Trevor in. He spoke softly to Trevor. The young man looked over at Ariel, then nodded. When they came forward, Hunter said, "The Metro officer is here. Your pack will be safe."

She stared into Sasha's eyes. He was going to be a gorgeous dog and would one day sire equally gorgeous Alaskan huskies. She handed him over to Trevor. "Thank you."

"Of course," he answered. "My mom wanted to know if you need anything."

"I'll call her later," Ariel promised.

Hunter cupped her elbow, and they walked out of the kennel building to greet the new police officer, a large, muscular man with a shaved head.

He made it clear he would not let down his guard. Hunter thanked him and then helped Ariel into his SUV.

On the drive to the hospital, she couldn't seem to sit still. Where was her friend? Where were Lance and Jared's accusations coming from?

Hunter's question—*what do they hope to gain by lying?*—bounced through her mind like a pinball ricocheting off one thought after another. "There has to be another explanation," she said aloud.

Hunter's jaw was set in a firm line. "You have to prepare yourself," he said. "Sometimes folks aren't who they seem."

She made a face. "I'm sure in your line of work, you see all kinds of horrible things from people. But I know my friend. We've known each other since our freshman year of college. There's just no possible scenario that would make me believe she did this."

"I *have* seen a lot of horrible things on the job. But I also know how hard it is when you love someone to see beyond what that person wants you to see."

Had someone he loved betrayed him? She was sad for him, but that didn't mean Violet was capable of such evil. "I'm sorry you were hurt by a loved one," she said. "But I'm sure this situation is different."

"Deception is deception."

"Just because someone deceived you doesn't mean that I can be easily deceived." Even as the words left her mouth, she recognized the pride in them. She winced. Was she fooling herself? Perhaps her ego was unwilling to entertain the idea of Violet's culpability, because it would mean Ariel had been a poor judge of character. She didn't want to contemplate that she was being obstinate out of pride rather than out of loyalty to her friend.

"Not me," Hunter said, claiming her attention. "My father."

She braced herself. "What happened?"

"Six years ago my dad fell in love. Head over heels, rainbow and unicorns, in love with a woman. He was too enamored to realize her true conniving nature."

"You did?"

"Yes. I had her pegged from the beginning, but my father wouldn't listen."

Which, no doubt, hurt Hunter and clearly made him wary of love. "She betrayed him?"

"Fleeced him of his life savings. And then planned to move on to the next unsuspecting mark."

Empathy bloomed inside her. She could only imagine how devastating that must have been for Hunter and his father. "*Planned?* I take it you intervened?"

Hunter glanced at her. His bright blue eyes reflected the soft glow of the dashboard lights. "Yes, I intervened. But not before the money was gone. I'll always regret that I didn't act sooner. She is now paying the price for her deception."

"But not everyone is like this woman," she argued. "That's like saying because one dog bites then all dogs are dangerous."

He brought the SUV to a halt in the parking lot of the hospital near the emergency room entrance. Then he turned off the engine and faced Ariel. "And if Violet is found guilty, then she will have to pay the price, too. Justice must be served."

A deep ache throbbed in her chest. "I agree that justice must be served. But Violet is innocent."

The look in his eyes as he popped open the driver side door made it clear he wasn't convinced.

EIGHT

When they arrived at the hospital, Ariel had to force herself to walk through the emergency room doors. Juneau brushed against her leg as if he sensed her hesitancy. She didn't want to be here. Not only because she didn't want to be poked and prodded again, but knowing she was going to face Lance and Jared and their accusations against her best friend had her stomach twirling like a weather vane on a windy day.

Hunter insisted that having her injuries checked out came before talking to Lance and Jared. She didn't protest, figuring it was better to get it over with. Hunter paved the way, dealing with the administrative process easily and pushing for a doctor to see her right away.

The doctor, the same one Ariel had seen the day before, scoped her throat and sent her off for imaging. When she returned, the doctor said, "It's a marvel that you're not worse off than you are. Whoever did this didn't quite know what they were doing. If they had, they would've been able to crush your larynx. As it is, they only managed to give you some mild bruising. Your throat will be sore and your voice a little hoarse for the next day or so, but you'll recover quickly enough with some rest."

Grateful for the prognosis, she said, "That's good news."

"For your sake, Ariel, I really don't want to see you again anytime soon."

"Believe me, I don't want this to become a habit."

After signing discharge papers and being given instructions on how to care for her throat, she and Hunter took the elevator up to the floor where Jared and Lance shared a room to recover from their ordeal.

An officer sat outside the hospital room door and stood as they approached. Hunter introduced himself and Ariel.

"Trooper McCord." He gave Hunter a chin nod of greeting. "Ma'am." He nodded to her. "My boss said I was to cooperate with the K-9 Unit."

The officer's gaze dropped to Juneau before he stepped aside to allow them to enter the room. The TV blared from where it was mounted on the wall. Jared and Lance each lay sitting up in their own bed. Lance, sporting a bandage on his head, had his smartphone out while Jared, whose arm was wrapped up in white gauze, stared at the TV. Both men's eyes widened and they sat up straighter when they noticed Ariel and Hunter.

"Ariel?" Lance exclaimed, barely audible above the noise of the TV.

Jared grabbed the remote control and turned the TV off. The silence was eerie as the men stared at her. Their faces drained of color.

Lance recovered from his shock first. "Ariel, you're alive!"

The two men glanced at each other, their expressions a mix of shock and disbelief, then looked back at her.

"This is so great!" Jared pushed himself up with his good arm. "We thought for sure you were dead."

A mix of anger at what they were saying about Violet and sympathy for the injuries they'd sustained swirled in her gut. "What really happened on the mountain?"

Both men looked to Hunter rather than Ariel. "We've already told the trooper, here, everything." Then Lance's gaze narrowed on her slightly. "How did you survive the fall? Jared saw Violet push you over the edge."

She shook her head and then decided that was not a good idea. Between the headache throbbing behind her eyes, the soreness of her throat and the ache in her heart, she really just wanted to leave, but this was too important. "It couldn't have been Violet."

"It was," Lance insisted, his face twisting. "She was out of control. She was having an affair with the tour guide and then she just went ballistic."

Ariel stepped forward. Hunter matched her step. Did he suppose that either of these two men would hurt her?

"She was *not* having an affair with Cal Brooks," Ariel ground out. A flush of outrage heated her face. "That's ridiculous. She didn't even know him until we met him that morning."

"Says you," Jared shot back at her. "We know what we know. She did this to us. And she did it to you. She's not a good person."

Ariel's fists balled at her sides. Her gaze zeroed in on Lance. "Did she tell you about the baby?"

Lance tucked in his chin and stared at her. "Excuse me? What baby?"

"She was pregnant with your child," she said as tears gathered in her eyes. "She had planned to tell you on the hike."

Genuine shock registered in Lance's eyes. He shook his head, winced and leaned back. His gaze drifted to the ceiling. "I didn't know..." His voice broke. "It's not my baby. It's probably Cal's."

"No! She was not having an affair. I don't know why you're saying this horrible stuff." Ariel glared at Lance.

He met her gaze with sadness in his eyes. "Violet isn't the person you think she is."

Her breath caught. "Don't say that."

Hunter stepped past Ariel. "Hold up a moment. You really didn't know about the baby?"

"No, I didn't know about the baby," Lance said. "If there even is one." He looked at Ariel. "She could've lied to you."

A fresh wave of frustration crashed through Ariel. "She wasn't lying! I was there when she took the pregnancy test. It came out positive. She's carrying your child."

Lance scrubbed a hand over his face. "If that's true—" He looked at Hunter. "If that's true, you've got to find her. You've got to get my baby prenatal care and whatever else it is that babies need when they're still in their mom. You have to find her and put her in jail before she hurts anyone else." He leaned back again. "I have a child…"

"You'll have to fight Mrs. James for custody once the baby is born and Violet is behind bars," Jared said.

Lance looked at him. "Fathers have rights."

The two men nodded at each other.

Ariel couldn't believe that they were concerned about custody issues. Wasn't anyone worried about Violet's well-being? This just couldn't be happening. "You two are wrong. Why are you lying? What is it that you have to gain from lying about Violet?"

"I'm not lying. My heart is broken. I love Violet but she betrayed me. Please, get out." Lance turned away from her. "Just leave."

Hunter took her by the shoulders and drew her backward against him. "Ariel, it's time for us to go."

"They are lying!"

Hunter drew her out of the hospital room with Juneau protecting their backs, nodded to the officer, and then put his arm around her shoulders to lead her toward the elevator. Fatigue and despair settled around her. She slumped against Hunter as the doors of the elevator shut. Tears streamed down her cheeks. "I can't believe it. I won't believe what they said about Violet. I know my friend. I know you might think I'm being foolish, but I'm not. I know my friend."

Hunter turned her so that she faced him and put the crook of his finger under her chin to lift her head until their gazes met. The tenderness in his eyes brought a fresh wave of tears coursing down her cheeks.

"When we find Violet, we will find out the

truth. Right now, my concern is you," Hunter said softly.

He sounded so sincere that she had a hard time remembering he was only doing his job.

"You heard the doctor. You need to rest," he continued. "I'm driving you home and you're going to take it easy."

A shiver of dread charged down her spine. "What if my attacker comes back?"

"I'm not leaving your side again," he promised.

As much as she wanted to take solace in his words, her practical side had her stepping back out of his reach and bumping against Juneau. "You can't just abandon your job to protect me 24/7."

"You *are* my job until your attacker is caught."

She wanted to protest and tell him she'd be fine without him. But deep inside, the knowledge that he and he alone stood between her and doom kept her silent. Bottom line? She had to put her trust in Hunter and faith in God to keep her safe.

Juneau nudged her and she stroked his head, finding calm in the soothing gesture.

The doors of the elevator opened to a clamoring of voices. The lobby of the hospital was crowded with news reporters. Several stuck their microphones in Ariel's face. Surprised, she drew away and grabbed Hunter's arm.

He used his other arm to block the reporters surging forward. "Everybody get back."

Juneau positioned himself in front of Ariel, a barrier that wouldn't be breached.

"Is it true Violet James murdered Cal Brooks and pushed you off a cliff?"

Stunned, Ariel stared up at Hunter. How did the media discover Lance and Jared's accusations?

Anger crossed his features. "No comment," he said gruffly. "Make room."

The sea of reporters stepped back.

"Let's get out of here," Hunter murmured.

Juneau led the way to the door.

"Did Violet James do that to your neck?" a reporter called out.

Ariel pulled the edges of her coat closed to hide her throat.

"Violet James is a murderer who tried to kill her soon-to-be groom and his best man," another reporter stated.

"She tried to kill you, her maid of honor. Don't you have anything to say?" someone else called out.

Ariel stopped in her tracks. The injustice of what was being done to Violet boiled her blood. She couldn't let these people ruin her friend's reputation. It wasn't fair or right. "I don't know what happened on that mountain. Nobody really knows. But I'm sure of one thing. My friend, Violet James, is not guilty of what she's been accused of. We are all innocent until proven guilty. Don't you forget that."

Flashes went off, stinging her eyes. Hunter's arm snaked around her waist and urged her out of the hospital doors to his SUV. The reporters followed them. He got her into the passenger seat and Juneau in his compartment. She quickly buckled the seat belt, cringing as reporters crowded around the SUV. Hunter climbed into the driver's seat, started the engine and eased out of the parking lot.

Thankfully, the reporters moved out of the way, allowing them to pass. Ariel glanced into the side view mirror. The reporters dispersed, some heading back inside the hospital, no doubt hoping to interview Lance and Jared.

Her breath came in shallow gasps and her heart thundered as if she'd just crossed the finish line of a race. Then, embarrassment replaced the adrenaline that had surged through her. "I can't believe I did that." She groaned and dropped her head into her hands. "I never do stuff like that."

His warm hand on her shoulder offered comfort. "Give yourself some grace, Ariel. You're upset. It's been a trying few days. You were defending your friend. And that is admirable."

She lifted her gaze to his profile. "But you suppose my loyalty is misplaced?"

"It's not for me to judge," he said. "My job is to protect you and to bring Violet in safely so that she can tell her side of the story."

She hoped and prayed that his commitment was real and that he wouldn't disappoint her. Who was she kidding? Disappointment was a part of life. Few people honored their word.

Hunter wouldn't be any different. And she'd be setting herself up for heartbreak if she allowed herself to believe in him. "Why don't you like hospitals?"

He slanted her a quick glance as if surprised by her question. "My mother died in a hospital. She was very ill for a long time."

Sympathy weighted heavily in her chest. "I'm so sorry."

"It was rough."

She could only imagine. And now here he was, taking her in and out of the hospital, which had to bring back the pain he'd suffered.

When they reached her house, Hunter hustled her inside. "I'll get Sasha and send Trevor home. You go do whatever you need to do to relax. We'll be in shortly."

Everything inside her rebelled at being told what to do. She wanted to deny that she needed him taking care of her, but the memories of her attacker grabbing her and squeezing her neck, trying to take her life, taunted her. She did need Hunter and she should be grateful he was willing to help her, even if it was only out of duty.

"Thank you, Hunter," she said. "It will be reassuring to have you here on guard."

Upon entering the house, she shivered at the quiet. Her attacker had robbed her of peace in her own home. She hadn't been this unnerved since Jason had lost his temper when she broke up with him. But thankfully, he'd left town and was somewhere in the continental United States or as Alaskans would say, the lower forty-eight.

She told herself to go into her room and change into her sweats, but she couldn't find the wherewithal to walk down the hall. So instead, she sat at the dining room table and once again bowed her head, folded her hands and prayed—for Violet, for herself and for Hunter. Unfortunately, she couldn't shake the dread gripping her.

The next morning, Hunter folded the blanket and stacked the pillow on the edge of the couch where he had slept the night before. He and Juneau went outside and released Officer Gorman, who had stood guard through the night, allowing Hunter to get some rest.

When Hunter and Juneau reentered the house, Ariel and Sasha came down the hallway. She wore well-worn jeans and a cable-knit sweater in a light pink that heightened the color of her cheeks and lips. Her skin was dewy from a recent shower and her blow-dried blond hair loose about her shoulders. Hunter couldn't deny how pretty and appealing he found her.

"Good morning," she said as she passed him to open the back door for Sasha. Her voice wasn't as raspy as the night before.

He hoped that was a good sign. "Morning."

The puppy clamored down the stairs and out to the snow-cleared grass, compliments of Trevor. Juneau stayed by Ariel's side where she stood watching the pup. "So, I assume you'll be taking off now?"

He raised his eyebrows as he stopped on her other side. Did she forget what he'd said last night? "24/7. I meant it."

She bit her bottom lip, drawing his attention.

"That's really not necessary," she said. "The attacker has come only in the dark. I'm sure in the daylight, I'm fine. You should go do your job."

"We've been over this." He wasn't sure if he should be insulted that she wanted to get rid of him or not. He remembered what his chief had said about Ariel being independent. Ariel wasn't used to having a human in her space. He got that. It had taken him a while to get used to living with his dad when he'd moved in after the debacle with that woman. Deciding not to push Ariel, he said, "I'm going to grab my computer and join a team meeting via video conference call." He turned to the door.

"There's ground coffee in the freezer," she said, stopping him in his tracks. "I keep it on hand for when my parents come to town."

He grinned. "That's good to know. Do you have a coffee machine or am I doing a pour over?" He could use a jolt of caffeine, though he'd already decided he'd try her tea.

"There's a machine in the cabinet next to the sink. My parents would never tolerate a pour over."

"How often do your parents visit?"

She shrugged. "Whenever they feel like it or there's a race in the area that they are working. They were here for the start of the Iditarod. I suspect I'll see them next in the fall, despite the fact that there's a race coming up this week. It's too small for them."

The race. She'd mentioned she was competing. He hoped by then the danger would be over and she'd be free to participate. "I'll get the coffee going and some water boiling for your tea."

The spring sun made her hair glisten, but it was her smile that enthralled him. He forced himself to focus anywhere other than on her mouth. The trees lining the property were dusted with snow, but the green foliage created a beautiful backdrop against a blue sky with fluffy white clouds. Quiet serenity surrounded them. He liked it here. So different than the two-bedroom apartment he shared with his father in downtown Anchorage.

Maybe that's why he'd slept hard last night. He hadn't had much in the last forty-eight hours.

He went inside and found the coffee and the coffee maker. Once the coffee was percolating, the aroma filling the house, he put water in the kettle to boil. Then he set up at the dining table and fired up his laptop. When the pot whistled, he turned the heat to simmer.

Juneau stood by the door as if he wanted out again. "Already?"

Hunter opened the back door, but the dog stayed in place, waiting for the release command.

"Release," Hunter said.

Juneau flew down the porch stairs, across the divide that separated the house from the kennel building and entered the open door. Shaking his head, Hunter followed him. Ariel was feeding her dogs. Each kennel door was open with each canine waiting for their breakfast. One by one, she placed a bowl of food in front of them, then sprinkled a white powder on the food. He figured some sort of supplement. She glanced up at Juneau as he skidded to a halt a few feet from the first open kennel. The beautiful gray-and-white Siberian Husky inside cocked her head at Juneau. Though their colorings were different, both dogs had a similar look about them.

Ariel paused with her gaze on Juneau. "I've plenty of kibble if you'd like to feed Juneau."

"He's got his own food," Hunter told her. "I'll feed him soon. We don't usually eat this early in the morning."

Her curious gaze met his as she put down the last bowl. "What do you do this early in the morning?"

"Normally, we'd go for a run on one of the trails of Westchester Lagoon. It's only a ten-minute jog from my downtown apartment," he told her.

She faced the dogs. "Eat." The dogs dug into their bowls. Then Ariel turned to him. "We'll be fine here, if you two want to take a run up the fire road."

Not likely. Hunter wanted her inside the house, not out here alone. Even with the dogs ready to sound an alarm, he planned to stay close. He glanced at his watch. "My conference call is about to start. Are you coming in?"

Annoyance flashed in her eyes. "Are you going to be monitoring my every move?"

Her independent streak was showing. If he

didn't get a handle on it, keeping her safe might turn out to be more difficult than he'd anticipated. Yet he had to admit to himself he liked her feistiness. There was much about this woman that he liked. And that might actually prove his undoing.

NINE

Hunter bit the inside of his cheek and held up his hands. He really had to get a grip on his attraction to Ariel. Treading lightly would be his best course of action. "Sorry. But I'd prefer to be in the same area as you."

She planted her hands on her hips. "I appreciate you being here last night. I'll admit I was freaked out. But in the light of day, I'm okay. I don't need a babysitter."

"Not babysitter. *Protector.* Big difference." Was she always this touchy or was she hangry? Neither of them had eaten breakfast. He could easily remedy that.

She shrugged, clearly unconvinced by his assertion.

"Let me make you some breakfast," he offered.

"I had a granola bar," she said. "You can help yourself to whatever you want in the kitchen."

Just prickly. Time to retreat, feed Juneau and get on the video call.

After grabbing Juneau's kibble and bowl, they went back inside the house. While his dog ate, Hunter snagged a granola bar from the cupboard and sat at the dining table where he had a clear view of the property entrance and kennel building.

Hunter logged into the video conference chat room and slipped his earbuds into his ears. Squares of live video popped up of each team member and his boss.

"Good morning, everyone," Lorenza said. "Now that we're all here… Hunter, why don't you fill us in on what happened last night."

He gave them the lowdown on the assault to Ariel and the drugged police officer, including telling the group about talking with Lance and Jared.

"Is Ariel okay?" Poppy asked.

"She is," Hunter assured his teammate. "A bit bruised and sore."

"Are the groom and his best man to be believed?" Lorenza asked.

Maya said, "There's no faking their injuries. But as to whether or not they were done by Violet James…" She shrugged.

"Hard to know at this point," Hunter agreed.

"Eli, what can you tell us about the satellite phone that was left in the cabin?"

The small square frame filled with Eli Partridge, the team's tech guru, showed him frowning and not looking into the camera.

"Earth to Eli," Will Stryker said.

Eli jerked his gaze to the camera. "Oh, sorry." He pushed up the bridge of his dark round glasses that framed his blue eyes. "The phone belongs to the parks and rec department. They reported it missing a week ago. They aren't sure how it ended up in the cabin where you found the groom and his best man."

The team went on to talk about the situation, each of them giving their thoughts and opinions. Hunter's gaze was drawn repeatedly to Eli. He didn't seem his usual, affable self.

As the call was wrapping up, Hunter said, "Hey, Eli. Is everything okay? You've been awfully quiet. More than normal."

Eli made a face. "No, everything is not okay, Hunter. You see way too much."

The comment elicited knowing nods from some of the other team members.

"Care to share with us?" Maya asked, her dark eyes round with concern.

Eli hesitated, then said, "If it's okay with the colonel."

Lorenza smiled. "Please, whatever is on your mind Eli, you can say it."

"It's my godmother. She was my mother's best friend. And the reason I came to Anchorage," he said. "She's sick. Very ill. Stage III cancer. She's only sixty-five."

Hunter's stomach clenched. He knew the heartache of losing someone to disease. His mother's death had left a scar on his soul. "I'm sorry to hear that."

"Thank you," Eli said. "Bettina is in a cancer care home, but they've told me that the treatments will soon stop having any effect. I was with her yesterday. And her most fervent wish is to see her only son and his family again before…" Eli swallowed and turned away from the camera.

"What can we do to help?" Poppy asked, her green eyes glistening with sympathy.

Having collected himself, Eli faced the camera. "I need to find her son and his family. All I know is that they are survivalists and may be somewhere in Chugach State Park."

The same park where Violet James was hiding out. Considering the park was one of the four largest state parks in the United States, many survivalists and those who wanted to remain hidden had plenty of space to do so.

"It's a big area," Gabriel commented. "Lots

of places where survivalists could camp out and not be seen, especially this time of year in the colder months. But with the summer months, it will be harder for them to stay out of the path of other hikers and campers."

"My ex-wife was raised by survivalists," Sean West volunteered. "She runs a mission in a remote area near Nome. I know that's far away, but perhaps she'd have some tips on how to find the family."

Hunter wasn't the only one to meet Sean's suggestion with raised eyebrows. It was well-known that he and his ex-wife, Ivy, were not on speaking terms.

"Are you willing to reach out to her?" Lorenza asked.

Sean nodded. "I am."

"That would be so appreciated," Eli said. "I'll owe you one."

"We all owe you, Eli," Helena said. "You've saved many of us countless hours and probably our lives numerous times."

There was a murmur of agreement among all the team members.

"That settles it," Lorenza said. "Sean, we'll wait to hear back from you. Eli, if you or your godmother need anything else, you let us know."

"I will, ma'am," Eli promised. "Thank you."

The meeting ended and Hunter clicked off. He

put his computer away and then he and Juneau headed out to the kennel building, but the room was empty. All the dogs' bowls had been cleaned and put away. He and Juneau followed the sound of Ariel's voice through the back door and off to the side, where there was a large fenced yard. And a specially made treadmill that was wider than the normal exercise equipment found in a gym was hooked to a sled that had been bolted to a concrete pad. No doubt that was how she trained the dogs to run together in a two-by-two formation when not out on the trail. He was impressed by her business acumen and her operation. There was much about Ariel that he found appealing.

He turned his attention to her and the dogs. All of the canines were sitting six feet apart. Curious as to what she was doing, he stayed where he was so as not to interrupt. Ariel threw a ball and called out a dog's name. That dog would chase the ball and bring it back to her, then return to its place. She called the dogs' names randomly until each had had a turn chasing the ball.

Beside him, Juneau let out a plaintive howl. No doubt his partner wanted in on the chase. But he wasn't sure how the other dogs would react to Juneau in their domain. It was one thing to allow him near while they were still in their kennels, but off leash and loose? He wasn't going to risk it.

Ariel waved. She released the dogs and all eight trotted off in various directions to sniff around the pen. He noticed none of them played with each other but stayed apart.

"Everything okay?" she asked.

"Yes, everything's fine." He leaned on the slatted rails around the dog yard. "What's on your agenda for today?"

"The dogs and I need to prep for this coming weekend's race," she said. "There are drills I plan to do. I was contemplating taking them out on the fresh snow—" Her voice had a distinct rasp to it.

He held up his hand. "Whoa. What did the doctor tell you to do?"

She made a face.

He waited, holding her gaze.

Blowing out a breath, she said, "Rest."

"Exactly."

She pinched the bridge of her nose. "Fine. I'll arrange with Trevor to come over and exercise the dogs."

"Good." He was glad she was willing to take it easy and let someone else do the work for her. "I could use some actual food. The granola bar was a nice snack." But certainly not enough to sustain either of them for long. If he made it seem that he needed the sustenance, then maybe she'd eat, as well. "And then I'm going to take Juneau for a run around the edge of the property. The crime scene unit will come back out here some-time today."

She grimaced and started walking back to-ward the house. "They came yesterday and didn't find any usable clues. They probably won't today, either. I feel bad dragging them out here a sec-ond time."

"They will come out here as many times as they need to," he said as he walked beside her. "That's their job."

Her nose wrinkled in a cute way. "I know. Just like it's your job to stay here to protect me and the dogs. But really, we'll be safe now. I can't imagine whoever attacked me would come back. And I don't for a second believe it was Violet."

"That remains to be seen," he said. "We don't know exactly what's going on. Better to be safe than sorry."

He'd made a promise to his boss and he was not going to renege on that promise. Ariel Pot-ter was going to be safe and he was staying put, whether she liked it or not.

Two days later, Ariel was about to jump out of her skin. Having somebody underfoot, in her space, wasn't comfortable. Add to that her growing attraction for this man who at every turn seemed to be there when she needed anything, whether it was feeding the dogs, cleaning the kennel and yard, locking up at night or preparing a meal. Though he'd slept on the couch the first night, she insisted he move his things into the guest room that her parents usually used when they visited. Much better than having him in the living room, should she want to get a drink of water in the middle of the night.

He was just so amenable and patient with her. She'd snapped at him on more than one occasion, mostly because she wasn't sure how to handle all the emotions he stirred in her. Gratitude, longing, frustration…affection.

Ariel couldn't help but smile at the image of him toggling his fingers at her and telling her to rest. She was tired of resting. Tired of the constant anxiety created by the threat of danger, waiting for the next time someone tried to hurt her. She kept telling herself the danger had passed, but Hunter wasn't convinced.

And to add to the pressure, she had a speech to write.

Tomorrow night was the regional awards banquet. The winners of the Iditarod and the runners-up would all be present, even though the official banquet celebrating the end of the Iditarod race had already commenced in Nome last month.

This banquet was for those who called Alaska home, and she would be receiving an award for the most champion sled dogs to come in the top fifty spots. She didn't quite know what she was going to say.

As she sat at the dining room table with a notebook and pen, Hunter came in and plopped down in the chair next to her, stretching out his long legs. He wore running pants and a thermal T-shirt that molded to his muscled and lean body. His hair was slicked back and his face glistened with a sheen of sweat. All that masculinity threw her off balance.

"What are you doing?"

Eyeing him, she wondered if he was always so curious. Must be a good trait in his line of work. "Trying to write a speech. The regional awards banquet is tomorrow night."

His chin dropped and his brow furrowed. "You are not going to an awards banquet."

She set the pen on the paper and faced him squarely. "Oh, yes, I am." She'd worked hard for this and nobody was going to deprive her of accepting that award. Not even this gorgeous lawman with control issues.

He made a noise in his throat that sounded

suspiciously like a harrumph. "I need all the details."

"Like what?" she asked.

"Place, time, the organizers' info. I'll need to make sure Eli, our team's tech person, has access to the video surveillance cameras."

"If there are any," she said. "You don't know what you'd be looking for. And I am certain whoever attacked me wasn't someone from the sled dog community. I thought you believed Lance's tale that it was Violet who attacked me."

"I'm reserving judgment."

That was welcome and unexpected news. "So you think Lance and Jared are lying?"

There was consternation in Hunter's blue eyes. "I didn't say that. I'm not sure what to think. The only thing I am sure of is you're not going anywhere alone."

Though the temptation to argue with him was strong because she would be among friends and wouldn't be in any danger, she choked back the protest and said, "Super. You can come with me. Do you have a tux?"

She couldn't keep the smirk from her tone. Not many men had a tux ready at the drop of a hat.

His lips curved into a smile that sent her heart pumping as if she had just crossed the finish line at the Iditarod.

"Yes, in fact, I do have a tux. I've been in a

few weddings over the years and will have my father drop it off." He grabbed her notebook and turned to a blank piece of paper. Then he picked up the pen and held it out. "Write down the details of this event, please."

Her mind turned from thoughts of his tux to the maid of honor dress hanging in her closet. A wave of worry crashed over her. Where was Violet? She missed her friend.

Taking a deep breath, she jotted down all the information that she knew off the top of her head about the award ceremony. Then she opened her laptop for any other details she'd missed while keeping half an ear on the one-sided conversation that Hunter was having with his father, asking him to bring the tux to her house.

It seemed she had a date for the banquet. She'd been on dates before so there was no reason for the flutter of nerves in her tummy. But she'd never had a date to something so public. Nor one she looked forward to with such anticipation.

The flutter died. So silly of her.

This wasn't a date. He would be on duty. Because someone wanted her dead.

The late afternoon sun cast shadows over the ranch. Was it a ranch? Hunter wasn't sure. Earlier in the day, he and Juneau had taken a few laps around the edge of the property on the lookout for anything out of place while keeping the house in view. Thus far they'd found nothing of interest. Nor had the crime scene unit when they'd conducted their search. "What do you call this place?"

Ariel sat in the recliner, reading a book with Sasha napping on her lap. Juneau lay next to the recliner and Hunter sat on the couch typing up his notes from the past few days. Or rather, revising his notes. Taking out his personal observations of Ariel. They had no place in his official report.

Looking at him over the top of her book, she seemed to ponder the question. "It's a ranch of sorts. But typically, when you say *ranch*, people assume you have horses or cattle. Most breeders say *dog kennel*. Then there's no question."

"Now that I believe."

His cell phone vibrated. He quickly scanned the caller ID on the cell before answering. "Hunter here."

"Hey." Will Stryker's voice filled the line. "We just got word from the hospital that Lance and Jared have barricaded themselves in an operating room."

"I'm on my way."

Ariel set her book aside and released the footrest on the recliner with a slam. Sasha awoke and jumped from Ariel's lap to race to his water bowl. "What's going on?"

"Lance and Jared." He was up and moving toward the hall closet, where'd he'd hung the clean uniform and tux his father had brought over.

That had been a strange visit. His dad and Ariel had hit it off right away. And before Dad had left, he'd pulled Hunter aside and told him that Ariel was *the one* and he'd *better not blow it.*

Shaking his head to dislodge his father's words from his brain, Hunter grabbed the clean uniform and then headed to the bathroom to freshen up and change. When he returned to the living room, Ariel was standing by the door with her shoes and jacket on and her purse slung over her shoulder. Juneau stood beside her.

"What are you doing?"

"I'm going with you. You might need my help."

Hunter hesitated. He certainly couldn't leave her here unattended. The Metro police hadn't any officer to spare the past two days, and Ariel's safety took priority over whatever Lance and Jared were up to. "I'll call Metro to see if Officer Gorman is available for a few hours. Once he arrives, then I'll head out."

However, when Hunter started his SUV a half hour later, Ariel climbed into the passenger seat and wouldn't be dissuaded from going to the hospital with him and Juneau. Figuring that the situation would most likely be resolved by the time they arrived, he didn't bother arguing with Ariel.

However, when they pulled into the hospital parking lot, the place was on lockdown. He showed his ID, getting him, Ariel and Juneau inside. They met Lorenza and Will on the fourth floor, and both of his colleagues had a dog by their side. Denali sat proudly beside Lorenza and a sleek-looking, black-and-white border collie stood next to Will.

The colonel's eyebrows rose as her gaze bounced from Ariel to Hunter.

"Ariel thought she might be able to help," Hunter explained. "What's going on?"

Lorenza's gaze turned speculative. "We're not completely sure," she answered. "The officer who had been stationed outside Lance and Jared's hospital door had been knocked out."

"Lance and Jared are claiming that it was Violet James," Will stated. "They say she tried to kill them, but somehow they managed to escape and for some reason barricaded themselves in the OR by pushing some of the bigger equipment inside against the door. Maya is checking with the hospital's surveillance videos to corroborate their story."

Ariel made a distressed noise. Hunter's heart ached for her. This had to be hard to hear.

Gabriel approached with Bear. The big, strong Saint Bernard outweighed the other dogs by at least twenty pounds. "The operating room has no other entrance points."

"The hospital is being searched," Lorenza said. "If Violet is here, we will find her and take her into custody, hopefully without anyone getting hurt."

Hunter glanced at Ariel, who looked like she might throw up. "Here, you need to sit." He directed her to a plastic chair. Juneau nudged his way between them.

The last thing Hunter needed was Ariel taking a nosedive. Apparently it had been a bad idea to allow her to come with him. He'd let his growing affection for Ariel affect his judgment.

A mistake.

One he wouldn't repeat, because there was no way he wanted to end up like his father, duped by emotion into making bad choices. It was time to guard his heart and put some distance between him and Ariel.

Ariel hung her head between her knees and took deep breaths as the nausea rolled through her. Juneau's warm body pressed against her leg. But not even his soothing presence could calm the riot of anxiety beating through her veins.

*Please, Lord, plea*se, she begged silently.

She wasn't even sure what to pray. Violet couldn't have done this. There had to be another explanation.

She sat up and looked at Hunter. "Has the guard come to? Has he confirmed it was Violet?"

Hunter looked to his teammates.

The trooper named Gabriel answered, "The guard is conscious. He said somebody came up from behind him. He didn't see who it was."

Ariel couldn't wrap her mind around the information. She buried her hands in Juneau's fur. "The guard must have left his post for somebody to be able to sneak up on him."

From the grim expression on Hunter's face, he'd come to the same conclusion.

Inside the operating room, the jangle of a cell phone going off rattled Ariel's nerves.

"We're hoping Lance or Jared will answer their phones," Lorenza said. "But so far, they aren't picking up."

"Is there an intercom system?" Hunter asked.

Lorenza turned to the hospital security guard.

"Yes. At the nurses' station."

Lorenza and Gabriel walked down the hallway to the nurses' station. After a few minutes, Gabriel jogged back. "They asked for Ariel."

"I can try to talk to them." She rose. "Maybe hearing a familiar voice will help them to feel safe." She could only pray so.

Ariel moved quickly toward the nurses' station with Hunter and Juneau keeping pace. Hunter deferred to his boss. The colonel nodded. He flipped on the operating room intercom.

Ariel gripped the mic. Her heart pounded in her throat, making her already sore vocal chords protest as she said, "Lance. Jared. It's Ariel. Please, come out. The K-9 team is here. They will not let anything happen to you."

Ariel waited a heartbeat, then tried again. "Lance, you know me. I don't trust easily, but I trust these officers. You have to come out and let them help you."

There was a commotion down the hall as the doors to the operating room slowly opened. Lance and Jared stepped out, wearing hospital gowns and the gray hospital-issue socks.

Ariel hurried away from the nurses' station and skidded to a halt with a small gasp.

Lance had a scalpel in one hand and a bed-pan in the other, held like a shield, while Jared had some sort of saw that he held like a bat. The white bandage around his upper bicep showed red seeping through from his wound.

"Violet's here somewhere." The green of Lance's eyes nearly disappeared behind his dark pupils. "You have to find her. She's evil, I tell you. She tried to kill us. Again."

TEN

A chill ran down Ariel's spine as she stared at the two men, who were clearly freaked out, claiming her best friend wanted to kill them.

It was so hard for Ariel to comprehend that Violet was some kind of maniac. But why would Lance and Jared make up such a story? She had to know.

Hunter's arm snaked around her waist and held her to his side. In a low voice, he said into her ear, "Let's get them disarmed first."

Juneau moved to stand in front of Ariel as if providing another line of defense. A warming sensation at the show of protectiveness from both man and dog chased away the cold that had filled her veins.

The three other dogs present stood beside their handlers and stared at the pair brandishing their makeshift weapons. An intimidating sight. Alaska State Troopers Will Stryker and

Gabriel Runyon stood ready to move, with one hand hovering over their sidearms.

Lorenza stepped forward, drawing Lance's and Jared's attention. Ariel held her breath, praying for the other woman's safety as she dealt with the two men.

"Mr. Wells and Mr. Dennis, I'm Colonel Lorenza Gallo of the Alaska K-9 Unit. We are here to help you, but I need you to put down those instruments so we can talk calmly, and no one gets hurt."

Lance and Jared shared a glance, then a nod, before putting down their weapons.

Will and Gabriel moved then, removing the scalpel and bone saw out of Lance's and Jared's reach before searching each man for any additional dangerous items.

Lance's gaze zeroed in on Ariel. He rushed to her side, his attention jerking to Hunter, then back to Ariel. "Ariel, we've got to go someplace safe. Come with us. We're leaving the hospital right now."

She pressed closer to Hunter. She didn't like the wild look in the other man's eyes.

"Hold on a second," Hunter said. "You two can't just leave."

Lance puffed up his chest. "We can do as we please. Jared and I are not prisoners or under arrest. We've stayed in the hospital because we thought we'd be safe. We're the victims here. My buddy and I are checking ourselves out and going where she won't find us."

"Yeah, that's right," Jared said. "We'll give you the location and a burner phone number once we're settled."

"Gentlemen." Lorenza held up a hand. "We can provide you a safe house."

"No offense, lady, but I don't know you," Lance said. "And I don't trust you. I don't trust *any* of you." His gaze settled on Ariel again. "Come with us, Ariel. It's the only way you'll be safe."

His fear was palpable, but there was no way she was going anywhere with him and Jared. Not only wouldn't she leave her dogs, but she wasn't going to forgo the safety of the K-9 Unit. "Lance, tell us what happened."

"I told you. Violet happened, that's what," he replied forcefully. "She came into the room with a gun in one hand and a knife in the other. She was going to kill us, but we managed to evade her. We barely escaped."

"That's right," Jared said. "Violet kept saying we had to die."

Ariel had a hard time wrapping her mind around the story the men were telling. Violet with a gun and a knife? No!

"I want my clothes." Lance spun away and

made a sweeping gesture with his arm. "Where are my clothes, my shoes and my house keys?"

"Me, too," Jared said.

"Your belongings are bagged in your room." A doctor stepped forward, his forehead creased with a stern frown. "You'll be leaving against medical advice. We still have tests to run and that gunshot wound needs to be monitored."

"It's better than being dead," Lance retorted. "We're leaving."

Ariel didn't know how to fix this situation. She didn't believe Lance and Jared's accusation that Violet attacked them, but they were clearly afraid of someone. But who?

A moment later, K-9 officers Maya Rodriguez and Poppy Walsh joined them.

"We searched the whole building," Poppy said. Stormy, the Irish wolfhound, lay down at his handler's feet, but Ariel could tell the dog was on guard by the way his eyes surveyed his surroundings as if searching for a threat. "No sign of Violet James."

"The hospital security cameras are working fine, all except for the hallway outside of Lance and Jared's room," Maya stated. Her Malinois, Sarge, remained standing, his tail high, indicating he was also on guard. "Someone had pulled the cable from the camera."

"See, I told you, she's a criminal," Lance said.

The nurse returned with two large plastic bags filled with Lance's and Jared's personal effects.

"Will, escort these two men to their room where they can change," Lorenza instructed.

Will and his border collie marched Lance and Jared away. Ariel stared after them. Had she just stepped into an old episode of some crime TV show that her father and mother used to love to watch when she was little? This just couldn't be happening.

"Gabriel, put a tail on Lance and Jared," Lorenza said. "For their safety."

"Yes, ma'am." Gabriel went to make the necessary arrangements.

"Did the hospital's video surveillance show Violet James in the hospital?" Lorenza asked.

"I had the hospital send the day's video feed to Eli," Maya said. "If Violet was in the hospital, he'll find her with facial recognition software."

Ariel was confident this Eli person wouldn't find Violet. She touched Hunter's arm. "You have to believe me, Hunter, this wasn't Violet. I don't know what's going on or who is after Jared and Lance, but it's not my best friend." Anguish tightened her chest. "She's in trouble. We have to find her."

Ariel refused to squirm under the scrutiny of Hunter's team as she held his gaze.

His blue eyes searched her face. "No one's giving up on finding her," he said. "There's nothing more we can do here tonight."

Not liking that he didn't believe her, Ariel nodded. She was tired and just wanted to go home.

Hunter urged Ariel toward the elevator and out to the SUV. She shivered as a new blanket of spring snow fell from the sky. As they drove away from the hospital, she leaned her forehead against the cool glass of the passenger side door and closed her eyes. Her head throbbed and heart ached. Nothing made sense. Could she be wrong about her friend?

She shut down the doubt. No, she couldn't be. The authorities would have to present her with irrefutable proof of Violet's guilt before Ariel would ever concede that she was capable of such violence.

Ariel's hands shook as she applied eyeliner to her eyes. She paused and set the applicator down to shake her hands out. "Come on, you can do this," she muttered to herself. "It's no big deal."

Sasha lay on the bathroom floor near her feet. He lifted his head from the chew toy. She used her bare toe to nuzzle him.

But this night *was* a big deal. She was going to the awards banquet, where she would be honored for breeding championship dogs. And she would be on the arm of a handsome man.

No, a handsome state trooper.

This was not a date. This was him doing his job, escorting her to the banquet to protect her. Nothing more. And she'd best keep that in mind before she let herself pretend that Hunter might have feelings for her or let herself admit she had growing feelings for him. It was all too much.

Taking a steadying breath, she finished her eye makeup, applied a light coat of pink lip gloss, and checked the mirror one last time to make sure the full-length black dress was okay with the colorful scarf she'd wound around her neck to hide the fading bruises.

Violet should be at her side tonight.

Ariel's heart clenched.

If her best friend was here, she would have done some fancy updo with Ariel's hair. Loose and straight was as fancy as Ariel knew how to do. If Violet was here, she'd probably lend Ariel one of her many ball gowns.

But Violet *wasn't* here. She was missing, possibly alone and hurt. Definitely afraid.

Ariel sent up a plea to God to keep her friend safe and to bring her home quickly. Ariel had to trust He was watching over Violet and her baby. Without her faith, Ariel didn't know if she could make it through each day, and she hoped that Violet was turning to God to see her through this ordeal.

Worry nipped Ariel as she picked up her handbag from the foot of her bed, slipped her feet into low-slung beaded heels and headed out to the living room with Sasha trailing behind. Her steps faltered as she caught her first glimpse of Hunter and Juneau. They stood side by side looking out the front window with their backs to her, like two sentries.

Juneau spun and trotted to her, wearing a cute little black bow tie nestled around his neck. Sasha jumped at him, trying to grab the edge of the bow, clearly wanting to play. Ariel scooped up the puppy and cradled him in her arms.

When Hunter turned to face her, his blue eyes flared with appreciation. Their gazes locked. Then her breath caught in her throat as she fully drank him in. His dark hair had been tamed back, his jaw was clean-shaven and his well-tailored tux emphasized the width of his shoulders. She couldn't help but sigh with delight when he came forward with a small square plastic floral box tied with a ribbon.

"Juneau's going with us?" Ariel asked in an effort to take the focus off the way her heart pounded in her chest over the fact that Hunter had bought her a corsage for the occasion.

"He is. There are very few places I go without my partner," Hunter said. "Hold out your left wrist." She tucked Sasha into her right side and extended her left arm. Hunter slipped the elastic band attached to a beautiful white gardenia over her hand and settled it onto her wrist.

He held her hand, his palm gentle and warm against her own. "You are beautiful."

Her mouth dried. She couldn't remember the last time a man, a handsome man at that, had told her she was beautiful. Certainly Jason never had.

Wariness reared in her chest. Could she trust Hunter's words? Or was he just being nice because it was part of his job?

"And you are quite handsome," she admitted, because she couldn't ignore the fact that she was drawn to him. She had to remind herself he was only accompanying her because he was doing his job. To protect her. To keep her safe. Not because he wanted to be with her.

The knowledge was like a drip of ice water down her nape, cooling her attraction and firmly putting her emotions on notice. *Do not fall for this man!*

Juneau nudged her leg, forcing her to break eye contact with Hunter. The minute she did she could breathe again. She crouched to scrub the Siberian husky behind the ears. Sasha squirmed, wanting to be set free. "You are quite handsome, too," she told Juneau.

"Are we taking Sasha?" Hunter asked.

She smiled and straightened. "No. I'll put him

in a kennel with the others. Trevor will swing by to feed them later."

"I'll let Officer Gorman know," Hunter said and moved to open the back door for her. "Do you have a coat?"

Her cheeks flamed. "Yes, of course." She handed him Sasha and went to the hall closet, where she donned a calf-length down winter coat.

After settling Sasha in his mama's kennel and locking up, she found Hunter waiting for her.

He held out the crook of his arm. "Your chariot awaits." He led her toward his SUV.

The shrill jingle of the house phone grated on her nerves. Her steps lagged a moment, but she shrugged and kept moving.

Hunter tugged her to a stop. "Shouldn't you answer?"

"It's probably a solicitor or wrong number. Very few people have the house landline number. I only have it in case of emergency. Sometimes call service out here can be spotty when there's a blizzard."

"Does Violet have the number?"

Her stomach sank, then bounced up into her throat. She hadn't considered that. "Yes. Yes, she does." Ariel hurried back inside the house. She picked up the landline's receiver, praying with all her might that she would hear Violet on the other end. "Hello?"

"Ariel, we saw you on the news," came her mother's worry-laden voice.

Her grip tightened around the phone. "Hi, Mom."

"I'm here, too, darling," her father said. "Are you okay? The news report said you were hurt. Should we come there?"

She closed her eyes against the onslaught of emotions pummeling her. "No. There is no need."

"It is true that Violet is a murderer?" her mother asked.

"No," Ariel ground out.

"But someone hurt you!" her dad exclaimed.

"Seriously, I'm fine. I have a protection detail keeping me safe."

"Yes, we read that, too," her mother said. "An Alaska State Trooper. We saw his picture in the *Anchorage Daily News*. You two looked very cozy together."

Ariel grimaced. "Mom, it's not like that." Great. She could only imagine how many other people had seen her and Hunter's photo taken at the hospital and would come to the same conclusion.

"Is the trooper there with you now?" her father asked.

Stomach churning with dread, she said, "Yes,

Dad, one of the troopers is here." No need to mention it was the same one as in the photo.

"I'd like to speak to him."

"Oh, no. That's not a good idea." The last thing she needed was Hunter interacting with her parents. Why would they even be calling? They'd shown little to no concern over her well-being during her childhood and adolescence. Even as the thought tore through her brain, she could hear her therapist telling her that was unfair. That love was shown through actions as well as words. They had fed her, clothed her and put a roof over her head. And they taught her about dogs. She would be nothing without that education.

"Dad, I'm on my way out the door," she said.

"Ooolı," her mother chimed in. "Hopefully on a date?"

She could just see her mother clasping her hands in front of her in hopeful anticipation. Her parents had been on her for years to marry and have kids. But dating hadn't turned out so well for her, despite wanting a partner, someone to share her life with. She should resign herself to the fact that she was better off without anyone getting too close.

"No, not a date." Ariel glanced at Hunter. One of his dark eyebrows rose. Heat infused her cheeks and she looked away.

"Then what is it?" her father asked. "What

have you gotten yourself into? You've always been a magnet for trouble, even when you were little. You'd wander off and get lost. I don't know how many times we had to go searching for you."

She bit the inside of her cheek to keep from commenting that she'd wander off because they weren't paying attention. And she couldn't remember them searching for her, only her being returned by some kindhearted person who had taken pity on her. Or her finding her own way home.

The only time her father took an interest in her was when she showed an interest in the dogs. Knowing they would badger her until she cracked, she decided to save the time and tell them, "The regional awards banquet."

"Ah. Good. I want to talk to the trooper," her father repeated in a voice that brooked no argument.

Ariel's lip curled. She didn't like when he used that tone. It brought back memories of her childhood. But whatever else she might think of her parents or how much she resented that she was never their priority, she was still the obedient daughter who loved her mother and father. Best to get this over with. She turned to Hunter and held up the phone. "They want to talk to you. Sorry."

His eyes were soft with empathy as he took

the phone from her. She walked away to go stand in the place where he and Juneau had stood earlier, looking out the front window. The Siberian husky joined her, leaning against the side of her leg. Her fingers tangled in his soft fur, liking the fact that he was tall enough and she was short enough that she could reach him without having to bend down.

Behind her, Hunter's deep voice filled the room.

"Trooper Hunter McCord. Yes, sir. You don't have to worry. I'm good at my job, sir. Of course. Yes. Yes, thank you." Hunter held the phone toward her. "Ariel, your turn again."

With feet laden down by imaginary sandbags, she walked back to take the phone. "Mom, Dad, I really need to leave."

"Of course, dear," her mother said. "Remember we love you and will be with you in spirit."

"But we can be there in person to fix this mess you've gotten yourself into," her father interjected. "You just give us the word and we will hop on the next plane."

Confused by the worry in their tones—where was this type of parental involvement when she was a kid?—and curious as well, she asked, "Where are you?"

"Nova Scotia," her father said. "Helping to organize a race team for the next season. We have some really good mushers here. I'm going to train a few and bring them to Alaska next year for the Iditarod."

"Good for you, Dad. I'll call you if I need you. And I really do need to sign off now."

She stood there for a moment after hanging up to collect her emotions. Why did they always have the ability to rattle her? She'd spent many years working with a therapist and her pastor to let go of the hurts of her childhood. Apparently it was time to meet with Pastor Thomas again.

A gentle hand on her shoulder startled her, and she jumped.

Hunter held up his hands in entreaty. "Sorry, didn't mean to scare you."

"Lost in my own thoughts," she said, not wanting him to feel bad on her account. "We should go."

This time as they walked out the door of her house, she was definitely leaning on him and she couldn't make herself stop. She needed his strength right now because the next few hours were going to take every ounce of bravery she possessed to willingly get up in front of people she knew and give a speech.

The drive to the banquet hall was quiet. Hunter turned on the radio to soft classical music. He wasn't sure exactly why Ariel's parents' phone call had upset her. But he sensed that she needed this time of quiet to pull herself together before she faced the people in her sphere at the banquet.

Affection for this brave and capable woman crowded his chest, making him dread the day that he had to stop spending time with her. He'd promised her parents he would do everything in his power to keep her safe, and he intended to keep that promise.

He pulled into the parking lot and halted beneath a lamppost. Cutting the engine, he angled toward Ariel. The soft glow of light coming through the front windshield glinted on her blond hair. "I talked with the organizer of the banquet hall, and he tells me there is no video security inside, but he's hired some extra security guards to man the doors and be on the lookout."

She blinked at him, a small V appearing between her pretty eyes. "On the lookout for Violet, you mean?"

He threaded his fingers through Ariel's. "Until we know otherwise, we have to operate on the premise that she is armed and dangerous."

"Maybe you do." She tugged her hand from his. "But I don't."

Her loyalty to her friend was admirable. And he found himself yearning for Ariel to have that same sort of faith and confidence in him. Maybe he wasn't so very different from his father. And that was a terrifying revelation.

ELEVEN

Hunter climbed out of the SUV and rounded the vehicle to offer Ariel his arm. She hesitated. Was she so angry with him for doing his job that she'd refuse his help?

Her gaze softened and she reached for him. He blew out a relieved breath.

Thankfully, the parking lot and sidewalk had all been plowed so she didn't have to traipse through the snow in her heels to the door. Then he released Juneau and leashed him up, and together they escorted her inside.

The banquet hall was noisy and crowded as they entered. They handed off their coats to the young girl at the coat check. Hunter noted that several different booths with vendors were set up in the outer lobby.

"Do you want to look at anything?" he asked Ariel.

She shook her head. "Not tonight. The vendors will all be at the race this coming weekend."

He refrained from commenting about the race.

When they stepped into the hall, a bright spotlight was suddenly placed on them. For a split second, all conversations dimmed. All heads turned toward them.

Ariel tightened her hold on his arm and whispered, "This way."

Scanning the crowd, Hunter let her lead him, weaving through the large round tables toward a table at the front of the room by the stage. A podium had been set up with a microphone, and right behind it was a hand-painted wooden backdrop depicting a beautiful winter landscape of the Iditarod.

People called out hellos to Ariel, and she responded with a gracious smile and acknowledgment of the speaker by name.

A woman with short, curly red hair and dark brown eyes stepped in front of them. She wore a slinky emerald-green dress, and the color reminded Hunter of Ariel's college sweatshirt logo and how cute she'd looked wearing her school colors.

"Ariel, who is your handsome date?" The redhead eyed him with an appreciative gleam in her eyes.

Beside him, Ariel stiffened. "Carly, nice to see you again."

"Likewise," she said, but her eyes were on Hunter. "Carly Winters. And you are...?"

"Ariel's date," he said. "Excuse us."

They skirted around the woman, only to be stopped again by a stout, balding man. He grasped Ariel's hand in his. "Miss Potter, we are so glad you're here. We were starting to think maybe you weren't going to come."

The veiled chastisement for being late wasn't lost on Hunter, nor apparently on Ariel, judging from her grimace. She extracted her hand. "I am so sorry, George. My parents called just as we were headed out the door."

The man's eyes widened and he nodded. "Ah." Apparently just invoking her parents' names was enough to explain away her tardiness. Her parents really must be something within the dog sled racing circles.

George's gaze turned to Hunter and then to Juneau. "I didn't realize you were bringing guests."

"I signed up for a plus one," Ariel explained.

Waving a hand, George said, "We figured that would have been Miss James, but since— well—" He waved his hand again as if to swat away a fly.

The hurt on Ariel's face ignited a low burn of anger in Hunter. He didn't like to see her upset. Or the fact that the world already considered Violet guilty. Only the results of their investigation would prove one way or the other. And they didn't have all the pieces to the puzzle yet.

"We will add another chair next to yours," George assured her with a pat on Ariel's arm.

Hunter narrowed his gaze on the man. "Are you the event director?"

"No, that would be Willa and David Ford," George said. "They are around here somewhere."

"I'd like to speak to them."

George gave him a tight smile. "I'll send them over. This way to your table."

Hunter stayed close to Ariel as they continued to weave through the crowded tables to one with a single empty seat. Hunter sensed Ariel's agitation as they waited for another chair to be brought to the table.

Pasting on a smile, she greeted the other six people sitting there and introduced Hunter and Juneau. He held out the chair for Ariel to sit, then took the seat beside her while the dog settled between their chairs. Juneau crossed his paws and rested his chin on them. Hunter knew the canine was not resting but watching. He trusted Juneau to have his back at all times. And now his partner would have Ariel's, as well.

Hunter leaned close to Ariel. "What's up with your parents?"

She unfolded her napkin and laid it across her lap. Bending toward him, she turned to speak into his ear, her soft breath tickling his skin. "What do you mean?"

Hunter glanced up to see if anybody was paying attention. Everyone had gone back to their own conversations. "I got the impression their call threw you into a little emotional chaos. And all you had to do was tell George your parents called, making us late, and all is forgiven? What gives?"

She leaned far enough away to meet his gaze. "Can we talk about this later?"

Her eyes held a plea and he couldn't refuse. He straightened. "Of course. But I'll hold you to that." He reached for his water goblet and took a drink.

Ariel did the same. She held her glass in front of her lips. "I have no doubt you will."

Ariel could barely choke down the deliciously prepared meal. Normally she liked these banquets because the catering company was stellar. But making small talk wasn't something Ariel enjoyed. She'd spent too much time alone as a kid with only the dogs as companions or later with a very small, select group of friends whom she was comfortable around. Most of her friends had either married or moved away. Violet would have been the last to get married. Ariel's heart ached. There would be no wedding to celebrate this coming weekend.

She was thankful that Hunter was adept at drawing out the other people at the table, though she speculated he was interrogating them with all his questions. If he was, he was very good at it. And when Willa and David Ford stopped by the table, Hunter stepped away to talk to the couple. She watched them until her gaze snagged on one of the catering staff. Surprise curdled her stomach. *Jason, her ex-boyfriend?* The man entered the kitchen and she shook her head, sure she was mistaken.

When Hunter returned to the table, his mouth was set in a grim line.

"Everything okay?" she asked.

He leaned to whisper in her ear, setting off a swarm of butterflies dancing a frantic jig in Ariel's stomach. She liked the way his aftershave mingled with his warm masculine scent. "Not as much security as I'd hoped."

"Are you worried?" Her nerves stretched taut, squashing the butterflies and making her limbs feel heavy. She doubted she could stand, let alone walk, even though she knew that very soon she was going to have to do both to accept her award.

"Irritated more than anything," he replied.

Hoping to calm her anxiety, she took the prepared speech from her handbag and looked it over.

Hunter stretched, putting his arm across the back of her chair, his fingers resting lightly on her biceps. Hot little spots of sensation fizzled her brain. The words on the page blurred.

Leaning in close, he murmured, "You're going to do fine."

She turned her head toward him and found herself not even an inch away from him. Her gaze dropped to his mouth and then back to his piercing blue eyes. A yearning she hadn't expected gripped her. She wanted him to kiss her.

Having his support meant the world to her.

Yet a tiny jaded voice inside her head mocked her. *Don't rely on this man. He'll only let you down as others in your life have.*

Besides, Hunter scoffed at love. And she wanted to believe that love was possible with the right person. She could only pray that God would reveal that person in time.

She shifted away from him, putting space between them. "It's easy for you to say. These people are not your peers, I'm going to make a fool of myself." Nervous tremors raced over her limbs.

His hand squeezed her shoulder. "No, not at all." He grinned. "Picture them all wearing party hats. I hear that works."

She rolled her eyes. "I'll have a hard time concentrating."

He chuckled. "Then just focus on me. I'm here for you, Ariel. I'm not going anywhere."

She swallowed as his words burrowed deep inside her, creating a longing that burst through her like a star erupting in the night sky. She didn't have anyone who was truly there for her. And while she trusted Hunter to keep her safe, could she trust him with her heart?

Unsure of the answer and horribly afraid to find out, Ariel turned to face the front stage as the award ceremony began. The first few awards were for the local mushers who had finished in the Iditarod.

As the seconds ticked by, Ariel grew more antsy. Her foot jiggled under the table. Juneau sat up and put his paw on her leg as if hoping to calm her agitation. Her heart melted. Dogs she could count on—they never broke promises or judged her and found her lacking. She reached down and ruffled Juneau's fur, taking comfort in the canine's presence.

Then they were announcing her name. Queasy with anxiety, she swallowed a gulp of cool water and laid her napkin aside to stand. Hunter's warm hand cupped her elbow, helping her to her feet. She gave him a grateful smile, fully expecting him to let go, but he didn't. Instead, he walked her up the stairs to the stage, making her feel cared for and special. She almost grabbed him to keep him at her side when he retraced his steps and took a position at the bottom of the short staircase, leaving her alone on stage.

With an inward groan, she chastised herself. This was all a sham. He was only in her life temporarily, doing his job. He wasn't her date, her boyfriend or even her friend. But her heart didn't want to believe that what they had between them was only about his job and the attempts on her life. Her heart wanted to connect to him, to bond and meld like a real couple. Once again, her desire to find Mr. Right reared, fierce and demanding. She squelched it. Hunter was not her Mr. Right.

But maybe for this moment, she needed to hang on to these feelings of being cherished, so that she could get through this speech without embarrassing herself. Then she would deal with the fact that she was letting herself get too attached to Hunter.

She stepped up to the podium and looked out on the sea of familiar faces. Yes, there were a few she didn't recognize, and it suddenly occurred to her maybe one of these people wanted her dead. She was certain, deep in her soul, that it hadn't been Violet James who had pushed her off that ledge, who had tried to strangle her and steal her dog. It could have been someone in this very room.

Panic sluiced through her veins. Her gaze jumped to Hunter. His reassuring smile and nod bolstered her courage. She could do this. He wouldn't let anything happen to her.

Her hands shook as she unfolded her speech. Juneau had moved to the bottom of the staircase beside Hunter. Ariel's gaze went to Hunter, and she mouthed *Juneau* and motioned for the dog to join her. Hunter's nod made her very happy. He whispered something to Juneau and the dog climbed the stairs and strode across the stage to stop next to Ariel, leaning into her side, offering her support. Her nerves calmed and she began to read her speech.

Hunter was so proud of how poised and articulate Ariel was as she humbly thanked the many people who had encouraged and supported her breeding business. She talked about the dogs from her kennel that had placed in the Iditarod and various other races throughout the last year, giving funny anecdotes about each of them. The room was warm and receptive to her. Hunter was glad to see her fear of embarrassing herself had only been pre-speech jitters. She had the audience enthralled.

A low, out-of-place noise underscored Ariel's voice. It took Hunter a moment to realize Juneau was growling deep in his throat. The dog had turned to face the wooden backdrop.

The hairs at Hunter's nape quivered with apprehension. He stepped up the first stair just as a sharp cracking sound jolted through the room. Juneau howled frantically, and then his teeth sank into Ariel's dress. The dog backed up, trying to drag her away from the podium.

Alarmed, Hunter bolted onto the stage. He wrapped an arm around Ariel, drawing her close to his chest, then took a step toward the stairs.

The backdrop collapsed, falling forward.

With Ariel in his arms, Hunter dove off the stage, landing with a thud on the floor between the tables. Juneau jumped clear as the backdrop crushed the podium where Ariel had been standing. Splinters of wood and debris rained down on Hunter's back as he covered Ariel, protecting her head.

There were gasps and screams as people scrambled out of the way. Hunter lifted his head, smacking it on the very tip of the backdrop. He winced, then whispered into Ariel's ear, "Are you okay?"

"I think so," came her muffled reply. "What about Juneau?"

He rolled to the side to find Juneau standing guard, baring his teeth at anyone who tried to come close. "He's good."

Gathering her to his chest, Hunter said, "We're going to scoot sideways until we're out from under this chunk of wood."

She nodded. Together they shimmied free. He stood and helped her to her feet. She leaned heavily into him.

"I've got you," he said.

Her hands flexed on his arms in response.

He looked around, searching for the three security guards who had been hired to protect the venue. Several seconds passed before he spotted two of the men wearing black long-sleeve T-shirts helping the guests closest to the stage and assessing injuries.

The third security guard hustled out from the back of the stage.

Hunter reached into the breast pocket of his tux and pulled out his badge, showing it to the guard. "What happened? Why did the backdrop collapse?"

The guard, a tall, muscle-bound man with blond hair in a man bun, said, "The backdrop's wooden supports had been rigged with small explosive devices. It looks like it had a remote receiver."

Hunter's gut twisted and a burning anger ignited his blood. Someone in the room had triggered the devices to go off while Ariel was onstage.

Not an accident. Another attempt had been made on her life.

He sent up a prayer of thanksgiving that Juneau had sensed the threat and gave a warning. It had been a close call. If Ariel had been standing there a few seconds longer, she would have been crushed along with the podium. The killer was getting bold.

"Call Metro PD. Don't let anyone leave. I'm going to take Miss Potter to a safe location. I want you to search this whole building for that receiver. Start interviewing everyone. See if anybody remembers seeing somebody behind the stage who wasn't supposed to be there."

"On it." The security guard moved away with a phone in his hand.

Hunter helped Ariel toward the exit and realized she was wincing with each step on her right foot. He stopped. "You're hurt." Why hadn't she said anything?

"My ankle," she ground out.

He had her take a seat in the nearest available chair, then squatted down and lifted the hem of her dress to see that her ankle was swelling, the straps of her sandal pressing into her flesh. "We have to get that looked at."

He helped her to her feet, then swept her into his arms.

"Hey," she gasped, clutching his shoulders. "I can make it on my own."

"Not on my watch," he said. "We're going to

the hospital. We have to make sure you didn't break your ankle."

She groaned. "I don't want to go back to the hospital. And neither do you. Can we just wait until tomorrow morning and I can go to my regular doctor at his clinic?"

"No," he said. "I'll be with you the whole way. We'll get through this together." A promise he intended to keep.

For a moment, she held his gaze, then nodded. "Hang on. I need my purse!"

Someone handed it to her. She murmured a thank-you and rested her cheek against Hunter's neck. Her vanilla scent teased his nostrils. He inhaled deeply. Something inside him shifted, and tenderness flooded his system. He liked having her in his arms. But the circumstances that had put her there twisted his chest into knots. He tightened his hold, wanting to take her pain away. To protect her for the rest of his life.

And that was almost as distressing as knowing he'd nearly failed to keep her safe tonight.

After retrieving their coats at the coat check, he carried her to the SUV and set her on the seat, tucking her dress and coat around her. Then he grabbed the seat belt and drew it across her lap, jamming it into the buckle. He paused as they were face-to-face. In the interior dome light he could see her eyes were wide, the pupils dilated.

"You're safe," he told her. "I'm not going to let anything happen to you."

She lifted a hand to cup his jaw. "I believe you. I believe *in you*."

His breath stalled in his chest. Ariel's words wound around him like a climbing strap around a tree, securing him to her in a way very little else could. Her faith in him was like an elixir to his jaded heart.

It would just take a slight movement for him to kiss her lush pink lips. Everything inside him wanted to give in to the attraction he'd been trying to ignore.

But she was fragile right now. Vulnerable. And he wouldn't take advantage of her. If he kissed her, he wanted her fully on board.

Yet he couldn't refrain from shifting his head to place a kiss on her palm where it had cupped his cheek. Her fingers flexed against his jaw and her eyes held his. The yearning, so bright in her eyes, enflamed the attraction arcing between them.

It took all of his willpower to straighten and step back.

"That's my girl," he murmured and shut the door.

As he rounded the front end of the SUV, his words echoed back in his head. Since when had he considered her his girl?

TWELVE

"Well, Miss Potter, you twisted your ankle."

Ariel breathed a sigh of relief at the doctor's announcement.

Dr. Chen looked at Hunter. "Will you be taking care of Miss Potter while she recovers from this latest injury?"

"I am," Hunter said.

The doctor smiled. "Well, that is very interesting."

Hunter tugged at the collar of his tux.

Ariel didn't understand what was going on between these two men, but whatever it was clearly made Hunter uncomfortable. If she weren't so exhausted and overwrought from tonight's ordeal, she'd tease Hunter. But all she wanted to do was go home. "Can I leave now?"

Dr. Chen looked to her, compassion in his eyes. "Of course. For the next twenty-four hours, ice and elevation."

She groaned. "*Seriously?* I am so tired of resting."

"Doctor's orders." Hunter gave her a stern look that was softened by the smile teasing the corners of his lips.

Her heart did a little flip. He was so handsome and attentive, she wanted to bottle up this fuzzy warm sensation for later when he was no longer a part of her life.

"I'll have a wheelchair brought over along with your discharge papers," Dr. Chen said.

After the doctor exited the exam room, Hunter took her hand. His palm was warm against hers. She curled her fingers around his.

"Do you have any idea who would've tried to hurt you?" he asked.

Her breath hitched. "You aren't confident that the person targeting me is Violet?"

"I haven't ruled her out," Hunter said. "But it seems like there's more going on here."

The ominous tone in his voice sent a shiver down her spine. She tightened her hold on his hand. "I don't know. I can't imagine anyone in the sled dog community would want me dead. I mean sure, there's friendly competitions between mushers and breeders, but nothing that would warrant these assaults."

An image flashed before her eyes. She bit her lip with dread.

Hunter squeezed her hand. "What is it?"

"I'm sure it's nothing." She hoped it was nothing.

"It could be something," he insisted. "Tell me."

Anxiety gripped her and she said, "I thought, maybe, I saw my ex-boyfriend working for the catering company. But I only saw him from the side for a brief moment."

Hunter's expression hardened. "Tell me about this guy."

"Jason Barba." Just saying his named produced acid in her gut. "We met about five years ago. He worked for the bank as a teller and he asked me out. He seemed nice and stable." She blew out a scoff. "We dated for over a year. But he wanted more out of the relationship than I was willing to give. He became very possessive, which was irritating and unnerving. So I broke it off with him."

That was an unpleasant experience. She shuddered at the memory. "He didn't take the rejection well. He made a scene every time I went into the bank. They finally fired him and he'd left town. But now, apparently, he's back."

"All right. I'll have him brought in for questioning." There was a hard edge to his voice.

Ariel's stomach twisted. "Could he be behind these attacks on me?"

"Only time will tell."

Though she hated the idea that Jason could harbor ill will toward her, especially after all this time, having another suspect was far better than assuming that Violet was trying to kill her.

The doctor returned with a wheelchair and post treatment paperwork. He also gave her a couple of over-the-counter pain pills that she washed down with a cup of water.

"Call if the pain becomes too much," Dr. Chen said. "I can prescribe something stronger."

"I'm sure this medication will be fine," she assured him. "It's just a sprain. I've had worse."

When she was settled in Hunter's SUV and they were headed to her property, he said, "You don't have to be in pain. It's okay if you need something stronger. You've had a horrible, rough couple of days. A head injury, a throat injury and now your ankle. That's a lot for anyone."

"I'm tough," she said, half joking. Though she was exhausted and could sleep for a week, she kept her chin up.

Hunter laced his fingers through hers again.

She liked this. Liked him reaching out to her and holding her hand. It made her feel loved.

The word reverberated through her heart and settled like a flower petal falling on snow. Soft and gentle. If she allowed herself, she could fall in love with this man. He was tender, kind and protective. He seemed to get her. Understand her. Something very few people did.

But even entertaining the idea of loving Hunter was foolish. He had no emotions for her beyond the duty to his job. She glanced down at their entwined hands. Could she be wrong? And if so, what did she intend to do about it?

Hunter carried Ariel through the front door of her house, hesitating in the entryway. Juneau paused as well, looking up at him as if asking, *what now?*

Good question, buddy.

Ariel had slid her arms around his shoulders and rested her cheek against the side of his neck. The tender affection crowding his chest was becoming familiar where she was concerned. He didn't want to let her go. But he had to. She needed to change into more comfortable clothes and put her ankle up.

She lifted her head and, using the soft palm of her hand, turned his face toward hers. "Is everything okay?"

He glanced down the lighted hall toward her bedroom. "Yes. Everything is good," he said, his voice husky. He slowly lowered her onto a dining room chair.

"I need to check on the dogs," she said.

"Trevor would have let them out for their last break, but—"

"I can do it."

"Thank you." She gave him a grateful smile. "You can leave Sasha with Skye."

"Okay. I'll be right back." To Juneau he said, "Stay with Ariel."

Juneau moved to her side in answer and made noises that sounded like he was trying to talk.

Hunter shared an entertained smile with Ariel.

Needing the cool air to bring back some sanity, he jogged over to Officer Gorman in his cruiser. After checking in and being assured all was well, he grabbed the crutches that Dr. Chen had insisted they bring with them out of his SUV.

Back inside the house, he helped Ariel to stand and adjusted the crutches beneath her armpits. "You need to get used to these for a few days."

Her light brown gaze snapped to his. "Twenty-four hours. Dr. Chen said twenty-four hours of elevation and ice. After that I am resuming my life. I can't keep sitting around doing nothing."

He got that she was a woman of purpose and liked to keep busy. He could only imagine how hard lying low was for her. But it couldn't be helped. "Off to your room to change into something comfortable. I'll get an ice pack ready."

She made a face. Then, using the crutches and her good leg, she hobbled down the hall to her bedroom. Just before she closed the door, he called to her, "Give a shout if you need anything."

Resting on the crutches, she turned to look back at him. "I will." Sparks danced in her eyes.

He shrugged, unwilling to apologize for his concern or his offer of help. That was why he was here and he'd best remember the reason.

She entered her room and shut the door behind her. Hunter scrubbed a hand over his face. He really should have asked Maya or Poppy to take over this assignment. He still could. If he were honest with himself, something he aimed for, he was growing attached to Ariel. More attached than he should, which was reason enough to find somebody else to take over this assignment.

However, he was loath to do so because, well, because he cared for the woman. There, he admitted it to himself. If anything happened to her and he could've prevented it…at least with him here, he would know that everything that could be done was being done to protect her.

His father's mocking voice inside his head jeered at him, *Arrogance is not going to get you anywhere, young man.*

Was he being arrogant believing he could protect Ariel? Maybe. But it was a small price to pay to keep her safe.

He found a large plastic baggie in a drawer and filled it with ice cubes from the freezer.

While he waited for Ariel to return, he called Colonel Gallo and gave her a full report of what had transpired that night.

"I'll have Brayden track down this Jason Barba," Lorenza promised him.

"Let me know if you find him," he said. "I want to be the one to question him."

There was a moment of silence before Lorenza asked, "Are you becoming personally invested in this case?"

Hunter sucked in a sharp breath, and he contemplated hedging the truth. But he knew the colonel would see right through him. "Yes," he said. "I am. But not so much that I can't do my job."

"Good to hear that. When we find this ex-boy-friend, we will let you know."

"Thank you, Colonel. I appreciate that."

He hung up and turned to find Ariel standing behind him, leaning on the crutches. She'd scrubbed her face clean of any makeup and tied her hair back into a loose ponytail, and she wore the college sweatshirt and sweatpants she had on that first night. So pretty his chest ached.

He cleared his throat. "You should sit." He held up the bag of ice.

She rolled her eyes and hobbled over to the

chair. He rushed to help her sit, popping up the footrest. Then he grabbed two accent pillows from the couch, tucked them under her ankle and placed the ice pack on top of her swollen foot. The whole time her gaze tracked his movements like a physical touch.

"Would you like water or tea?" He pivoted toward the kitchen, but she snagged his hand, stopping him before he could move away. Her eyes were wide and full of trust and some other emotion that made his blood quicken.

A small smile on her lips drew his attention to her words.

"I know I've asked this before, but why are you being so kind to me?" She tilted her head. "It's almost as if you care."

His heart squeezed tight. He wouldn't lie to her. "I do care, Ariel. Someone's trying to hurt you. I'm not going to let them."

She tugged him closer so that he had to crouch down next to the side of the chair. Curiosity burned in his chest.

Releasing his hand, she twisted so that she could reach up and cradle his jaw, claiming his focus with her eyes. "I can't tell you how much your presence here means to me. How much you mean to me."

His mouth went dry. Her words and the sweet

vulnerability in her gold-dusted eyes filled him with awe. His gaze dropped to her lips, then lifted back to her eyes.

"Hunter," she whispered.

There was so much in the way she said his name. A plea, a question, a demand. Did he dare kiss her? Did he dare refuse?

Who was he kidding? He could no more refuse her than he could stop breathing. Leaning forward, he pressed a kiss against her mouth. Her hands slid into his hair, gripping his head, pulling him closer.

The kiss deepened, and sensation rocketed through him, streaking along his nerve endings and making the world fade. Then her lips softened beneath his and tender emotions burned the backs of his eyes. They drew apart and he pressed his forehead against hers to let his heart rate calm and his breathing even out.

Eventually he leaned back on his heels, away from her, forcing her to let him go. "Ariel—" he began, not sure what, exactly, he intended to say. "I'm—"

She pressed a finger to his lips. "Let it be."

Let it be? Confusion clouded his brain. She didn't want to talk about that incredible kiss?

Sitting back into the recliner and turning her face away from him, she said, "I'll sleep here tonight. Do you mind turning off the lights?"

"I'll turn all but the kitchen light off." He straightened. "You won't be sleeping out here alone. Juneau will be right here."

"I appreciate both of you looking out for my safety."

The trust in her eyes brought a lump to his throat. He swallowed and undid the constricting bow tie at his neck. "You should rest."

A soft smile touched her lips. "You looked very handsome tonight. Everyone—well—every woman in the banquet hall thought so."

He didn't care what anyone else thought. All he cared about was the fact that she found him handsome.

He spun away and strode to the guestroom. Okay, maybe his boss was right to question how personally involved he was getting in this case, how personally involved he was becoming with Ariel.

Was he losing perspective? Exercising bad judgment because he'd let down his guard and let Ariel in?

Ariel awoke warm yet stiff from sleeping in the recliner. A thick blanket had been put over her, but her foot was cold still. She glanced down to note that the ice bag had been refilled with new ice. Joy spread through her chest at his tender consideration.

Juneau sat beside the recliner, staring at her as if waiting for her to awaken. Her heart melted. Both man and beast were taking such good care of her.

She closed her eyes and relived the kiss.

So much better than she'd imagined it would be. And everything she'd hoped for. She hadn't planned on kissing him, but she'd been so emotional and had needed the connection.

Had it affected him as much as it had her?

She longed to talk to Violet right now. Her best friend would help Ariel process the overwhelming emotions swamping her.

She lifted up a prayer for Violet, praying she'd be found soon. Alive and well. It hurt to the core to consider her friend might be injured or worse.

Juneau whined as if wanting her attention. She scrubbed the dog behind the ears.

"Where is your handler?" she asked.

Juneau cocked his head, and then his gaze went to the back door.

Was Hunter letting her dogs out of their kennels?

Ariel tried to reach the crutches, but they were just beyond her fingertips, so she sat forward to remove the ice bag and set it on the arm of the recliner. Then, leaning down to release the footrest while keeping her injured ankle elevated, she scooted to the edge of the recliner and stretched as far she could to grab the crutches. It wasn't easy to maneuver them beneath her armpits, but she managed it and used her good leg to stand upright. Her ankle throbbed for a moment, then settled down.

She blew out a breath.

Between her head, her throat and her ankle, she didn't know what else anybody could do to her. Dread camped out in her chest. They could kill her.

She hobbled to the bathroom, and when she returned to the living room, Hunter was in the kitchen while Juneau ate his kibble.

"Are you doing okay?" he asked.

Seeing him making himself at home in her kitchen filled her with an odd and wonderful sense of contentment. "I am. The dogs?"

"I let them all out one by one so they could do their business and have a moment to chase the ball. And then I called Trevor. He'll be here soon to feed them. You need to get back in the recliner."

She growled, then regretted it as the reverberation hurt her throat. "You're going to take this twenty-four-hour thing seriously, aren't you?"

He grinned. "Of course. I found eggs in your refrigerator and some spinach. I'll make a scramble."

Her stomach rumbled, reminding her she

hadn't eaten much of the dinner at the banquet. "There's bread in the freezer for toast."

"You keep your bread in the freezer?"

"I buy the organic, non-preservative kind. If I leave it out, it goes bad too quickly before I can eat it all."

"Makes sense."

She hobbled back to the recliner and got herself situated. Before she could blink, Hunter was there, tenderly lifting her ankle to slide the pillows under it. He grabbed the ice pack and gently laid it over the top of her ankle.

She'd embarrassed him last night with her thanks and her kiss. Or maybe he was overwhelmed, like she was? Either way she didn't regret kissing him. Ariel had never had anyone pamper her like this, making her feel special. She didn't care that it was part of his job. For now, he was here, and she was going to enjoy every moment of it.

THIRTEEN

Ariel sat on the edge of her bed and tested her injured foot on the third morning after the near miss of being crushed by the banquet hall backdrop. She chalked up her restless nights of sleep to the pain in her foot, but it was probably more the lingering fear. And no way would she admit to being kept awake by her growing affection for Hunter.

She was falling for him and there wasn't much she could do about it. Except keep the knowledge to herself if she hoped to prevent being hurt when his assignment to protect her ended.

Today, she was done sitting around babying her foot. After the first twenty-four hours had passed, she'd been unable to bear much weight on that leg. Hunter had insisted she continue to heal with rest. She'd grumbled but had to admit it was really nice to have him caring for her. Her head no longer throbbed, her throat was better and the swelling in her ankle had gone down so much that her foot looked normal.

It was time to resume her life. She had a race to prep for. Ariel had confidence that her dogs would do well. If she placed in the top four positions, she'd make a bit of money to keep things afloat until the next race or next litter of puppies.

First, though, she had to be able to stand and walk on her own, without the crutches or leaning on Hunter. Slowly, she put weight on her injured ankle. Tender, but doable.

Sasha nipped at her toes as she put on her socks. She tossed a small stuffed toy for him to tackle while she managed to put on a pair of sturdy hiking boots that would support her ankle. Determined Hunter was not going to thwart her effort to exercise her dogs, she squared her shoulders and left her room. However, Hunter and Juneau were not in the house. They must've gone for a run. Something that had become their routine each morning.

She made herself a cup of strong black vanilla bean tea and put it in a thermos. After feeding the dogs and giving them their supplements, she released them to the outside fenced area. She contemplated hooking the dogs up to a sled and heading down the fire road, but the recent events kept her from doing what she normally would. Frustration bit into her like a rabid dog.

Ariel wanted her life back to normal. She wanted her best friend home and well. And she wanted to not be afraid to go about her day. But the reality was, she had to be patient. A feat that seemed insurmountable at times.

An odd tingling at the base of her neck had her searching the trees beyond the fence marking the property boundary. Was someone watching her? A shiver of fear raced down her spine.

Movement in her peripheral vision jolted her heart rate, and a small gasp escaped her as Juneau came bounding around the corner of the kennel building. Her heart calmed from the momentary fright but sped up for an entirely different reason as Hunter came into view, striding purposely toward her. He had on running pants, a long-sleeve T-shirt and a beanie over his dark hair.

"You should have waited for me," he said, clearly displeased.

Glancing at the trees, she nodded. "Sorry. I was anxious to get out of the house."

"The ankle is better?"

She lifted her foot and rotated her ankle. "Yep."

Hunter's phone rang. He grabbed it from the pocket of his running pants. "I have to take this." He headed toward the house. "Are you coming?"

"Yes, I'll be right there." She allowed him a head start to give him privacy on his call.

He opened the back door and Sasha escaped the house, shooting past Hunter and Juneau to race toward Ariel.

Laughing, she squatted down to wait for the puppy to reach her. A sharp crack echoed through the trees, startling her. The wood railing next to her head splintered. For a heartbeat, she froze. Then realization stole her breath.

Gunfire. Someone was shooting at her.

She hobbled forward as fast as she could with her injured ankle, the pain a small price to pay. More shots were fired, the loud sound reverberating through the air. Bits of gravel, dirt and snow flew from the impact of the bullets hitting the ground close to her feet. She released the dogs from the pen and pointed to the house. "Inside!"

Sasha yelped, his little body quivering. Her heart leaped in her throat. She scooped up the puppy just as Hunter tore out of the house, running toward her.

She gestured wildly. "Go back!"

But he didn't. Instead, he wrapped her and Sasha into his arms, using his back as a shield, and hurried them inside the house behind the other dogs.

"Somebody's shooting at me." Her disbelief made her mind sluggish.

"You and the dogs get down!" He pushed her underneath the dining table. "Stay here."

With his sidearm in hand, Hunter and Juneau ran out the back door.

"No!" she protested, afraid they'd get hurt. But he was gone. She gathered the dogs close, burying her nose in Sasha's fur.

She waited for a long moment. Dread choked her. She couldn't let Hunter be out there alone. What if the person shot him? Or Juneau.

Terror sliced through her, leaving a bleeding trail. She needed to call for backup. Decision made, she crawled out from underneath the table, keeping the puppy close to her body like a football and herding the dogs to stay at her side. Then she grabbed the house phone, hurried into the bathroom and closed the door.

Dialing 911, she prayed Hunter would return to her safely.

Hunter ran in a crouch as he and Juneau headed off to the southwest corner of the property, where he was pretty sure the shots had originated. There was no cover for him or Juneau. He kept to the fence built on the property line. Then he took a breath, sent up a prayer for safety and bolted over the wooden fence. Juneau climbed underneath the rails. In the woods of spruce and aspens, the assailant crashed through the underbrush, not even trying for stealth. Juneau ran ahead of Hunter, leading the way toward the fire road.

The slam of a vehicle door followed by the roar of an engine ground Hunter's teeth together. The intruder was gone by the time he broke through the trees to the snow-packed road. And he noted that the barricade the police had erected had been dismantled. Hunter whistled to bring Juneau back; he didn't want the dog following the suspect's vehicle out onto the highway.

Now there was no question whoever had been targeting Ariel was using the fire road. He curled his fingers into fists.

Picking his way back through the trees, Hunter used his phone to report the incident and say that the shooter was gone. He learned Ariel had already made the call. Admiration for her spread through his chest. The woman had so much grit and spunk, compassion and kindness. She was also loyal and pragmatic. Stubborn. One of a kind. He was falling hard for her.

The realization made him stumble over a root.

Juneau's barking diverted Hunter's attention from his inner turmoil. He picked up speed, eating up the ground until he found the dog sitting next to a tree. On the ground at his feet lay a baseball cap. He removed a dog waste bag from his pocket and used the edge of it to pick up the hat so that he didn't contaminate the evidence. Then, searching the ground, he spotted three shell casings. He gathered those in the bag as well, careful to keep from handling them too much.

When he and Juneau arrived back at Ariel's house, he found her locked in the bathroom.

"Ariel, you're safe," he called to her through the door as he slipped on a fresh T-shirt.

The door flew open, dogs poured out and she threw herself into his arms. He held her against him. Emotions crashed through him. Affection. Joy. Relief. And then a fierce wave of frustration that this perp almost killed her pounded at his temples. He had to do a better job of keeping her safe.

She leaned away from him. "I was so worried. I was afraid that you would be shot."

He gave her a smile he hoped was reassuring. "I'm made of Teflon."

Her mouth thinned. "No," she said. "You're not. You're flesh and blood. And you're in danger by being here."

His arms tightened around her. "Danger is a part of my job, Ariel."

She dropped her gaze and leaned her head against his chest. "I know. And it scares me."

With the crook of his finger, he lifted her chin. "Ariel, I know you believe and trust God."

She nodded, her eyes never leaving his.

He cupped her cheek with his palm. "Then you have to trust that He will protect both of us."

For a moment, she stared at him. Then her hand slid around his neck and pulled him close until their lips met. She kissed him deeply, tenderly, and his heart swelled with more emotions than he could handle.

When she pulled away, she smiled. "Thank you for that reminder. I do trust God. And I trust you."

She let him go and walked toward the living room, leaving him standing there, stunned. He hadn't understood until this moment how much her trust meant to him. It was everything. *She* was everything. Boy, he was in trouble.

"I called for backup," she said over her shoulder. "They should be here soon."

That was just what he needed to galvanize him into action. He joined Ariel on the front porch. She'd put the adult dogs back in the outdoor pen and now cradled Sasha in her arms. Juneau sat beside her. Moments later, a Metro police cruiser arrived with lights flashing and parked, followed by an Alaska K-9 Unit vehicle.

Poppy Walsh and Stormy jumped out of the vehicle and hurried to confer with the police officers.

Hunter and Ariel met the trio in the driveway.

Quickly he explained the situation as the officers took notes. "There are spent bullets here in the drive. And I have a baggie of shell casings I found in the woods."

"We'll find the bullets," the older of the two officers said.

As soon as the officers moved away, Poppy gave Ariel a kind smile. "Are you okay?"

"I am now," she said. "I shouldn't have left the protection of the house. When is this going to end?"

Hunter put his arm around her waist. "Soon."

Ariel glanced up to meet his gaze as she leaned against him. "You can't promise that."

No, he couldn't, but he wanted to. He wanted to keep this woman safe, to keep her close and to tell her—

Poppy cleared her throat, her eyebrows raised.

Hunter dropped his arm from around Ariel as a heated flush crept up his neck. "Let's take this inside. I have something to show you."

He led the way into the house.

"I've interviewed Mrs. James and the people who work at the estate where Violet lives with her mom," Poppy said.

"And they told you the same thing I did," Ariel said with confidence. "Violet wouldn't hurt anyone."

"Yes, that is the same thing I've heard from

everyone who knows her," Poppy confirmed. "Everyone except her fiancé."

Ariel made a scoffing noise.

"I've also interviewed the groom's family," Poppy said. "Lance's parents, Ann and Carl Wells, say he's a wonderful son and are very concerned for his well-being."

"And the other people in his life?" Hunter asked.

"Here's where it gets interesting," Poppy went on to say. "His ex-girlfriend, Leah Orr, has a completely different story. She says he lies easily. She caught him in several over the course of the six months they dated, and he ended their relationship when an inheritance she was supposed to get didn't pan out."

"What kind of lies?" Hunter asked.

"She didn't go into specifics," Poppy said. "I had the impression the lies weren't anything big enough to cause her to break it off."

"Violet didn't know about the ex-girlfriend," Ariel interjected. "At least, she never mentioned her to me. Have you interviewed Lance's sister, Tessa Wells? She and Lance weren't on speaking terms. Violet was hoping to meet her before the wedding."

"She's out of the country. But I talked to a couple of her friends who said that she didn't think too highly of her golden boy brother. I will make sure to interview her when she returns."

"And what about Jared?" Hunter asked.

"Will's been looking into him," Poppy said. "The last I heard, he was having trouble finding anyone willing to talk to him about Lance's best man. Apparently he doesn't have family. Kept to himself when out on the commercial fishing boats."

"That's right," Ariel said. "I remember Violet mentioning that Jared grew up in foster care."

"Ariel, what did you think of Lance?" Poppy asked.

Hunter was also interested to know. She'd never spoken a bad word about her best friend's fiancé, though she'd denied their claims that Violet was violent.

Ariel made a face. "Well, to be honest, I have never really liked Lance. Or Jared, for that matter. But Lance made Violet happy so I had to be happy for her."

"What about Lance and Jared did you not like?" Hunter asked.

"There was nothing overt that I could put a finger on. Just little subtle things. Like when we would go out to eat as a group or go anywhere, really, Lance made all the decisions. He rarely consulted Violet or any of us for an opinion. I think Violet felt taken care of, maybe?" Ariel shrugged. "Her father was a commanding, run-the-show kind of man."

Hunter had no doubt that Lance's behavior would grate on Ariel. She was too independent to let any man choose for her. He liked that independent spirit. "And Jared?"

She shrugged. "Nothing I can articulate."

"You said you had something to show me," Poppy reminded him.

"Yes." He moved to the dining table and showed her the ball cap and bullet casings.

Ariel let out a little gasp.

Hunter narrowed his gaze at her "You recognize this hat?"

"Not the hat specifically," she said. "That's Carly Winters's logo."

The name sounded familiar, but he couldn't place it. "And who is she?"

Disbelief shone in her eyes as she stared at him. "The redhead you met the other night."

An image flashed in his mind of a woman in a green dress. "Right," he said. "The woman who talked to us at the banquet hall. Is there a story there between you two?"

Ariel blew out a breath. "Not between us, per se. She moved here about a year and a half ago and started a breeding program."

"So basically, she's your competition?" Poppy asked.

"Technically, yes," Ariel said.

"Why didn't you mention her before?" Hunter mentally added Carly Winters to his list of suspects. Now they had three. Her ex-boyfriend, Jason, a competitive breeder named Carly, and Ariel's best friend, Violet. Which one of them wanted her dead?

"I didn't want to speak ill of her. It would sound like sour grapes," Ariel said with concern in her eyes.

"Is she breeding Alaskan huskies, as well?" he asked.

"She is."

Could this other breeder want to do away with her competition? Hunter wanted to talk to this woman. "Are her dogs as good as yours?"

"It's too soon to tell," Ariel said.

"Could she be jealous of you?" Poppy asked.

"I don't know." Concern lanced across Ariel's face. "We don't socialize."

Hunter doubted Ariel socialized with very many people because she was so focused on her dogs and her business.

"Carly has been wanting to buy one of my adult dogs since she arrived in town," Ariel said. "I've always said no because I'm not ready to retire any of my breeding dogs and I'm not going to sell a still viable dog to my competition. But, that said, I don't see her doing this."

Of course she didn't. Ariel tended to see the good in people. Hunter wasn't so inclined. "Poppy, do you mind taking the evidence to Tala and see if she can get any kind of DNA or prints that we could use?"

The forensic scientist was the best in the state. Hunter knew if there was anything to find, she'd find it.

"Of course," Poppy said. "Do you have a brown paper bag I could carry this in?"

Ariel found one, and then they walked Poppy outside.

The two police officers held up an evidence bag containing three spent bullets. Poppy had them place the plastic bag inside the brown paper bag.

"Can you have Tala run the ballistics against the bullet we found in Cal Brooks?" Hunter asked.

"I sure will." Concern darkened Poppy's green eyes. "What are you two going to do?"

Hunter contemplated Ariel's comment that Carly wanted to buy a dog. "You mentioned before that you have people requesting to purchase your dogs."

Ariel nodded. "I have people all over the place who contact me about buying the puppies."

"We are going to pay Carly Winters a visit," Hunter decided because the woman was local, but was she out to hurt Ariel? "I'll ask the police officers to stay here until we return. Just to make sure no shenanigans happen while we're gone."

Surprise flared in Ariel's eyes. "I need to put the pack away. I'll be right back."

Hunter watched her walk away, glad to see she wasn't limping. He spoke to the officers, who agreed to stay until he and Ariel returned.

"What should I tell the colonel?" Poppy asked.

"Tell her there's something else going on here. That these attacks on Ariel aren't being done by Violet James."

Poppy titled her head. "And what are you speculating about the attacks on Lance and Jared?"

"Two different cases," he said. "It could very well be Violet who is after Lance and Jared. But she's not the one targeting Ariel."

Poppy nodded. "I agree. Do you want me to accompany you to Carly Winters's place?"

Hunter didn't hesitate. "Actually, yes, that would be appreciated."

With Poppy following them and Ariel giving directions, Hunter drove to the Winters Kennels. The place wasn't as big as Ariel's property. A small two-story house stood off to the side of what Hunter suspected was the kennel building and a dog run. Hunter glimpsed movement at the window.

Someone was home. He knocked on the

front door. A few moments later, the redheaded breeder opened the door.

Her dark brown eyes widened. "You were with Ariel at the banquet."

"That I was," Hunter replied. "Trooper Mc-Cord. I have a few questions for you."

She frowned, her gaze going over his shoulder. "What is this about?"

"We found a ball cap with your logo on it at a crime scene," Hunter said, watching the woman closely.

Surprise flared in her eyes. "Okay. That has nothing to do with me." She leaned against the doorjamb and crossed her arms over her chest. "Lots of people have my hats. I give them out at races and events. Is she accusing me of something?"

"No, ma'am," Hunter said. "We're just asking some questions."

Carly's gaze went to Ariel. "Right. You're just afraid that I'll take away from your business so you're making trouble for me."

Ariel climbed the steps to stand beside Hunter. "Carly, that's not it at all. We just want to know who might have left the ball cap behind on my property."

Her lips twisted. "I don't know."

"Were you giving the hats out the night of the banquet?" Ariel asked.

"Yes," Carly said. "That's not a crime."

Hunter exchanged a glance with Ariel. Could her ex-boyfriend have picked one up? "No, it's not a crime. Do you own a gun?"

Carly's eyebrows dipped low. "A rifle. I'm a woman alone out here. There's plenty of predators to warrant the caution."

Hunter couldn't argue with that. He'd have to run a license check to see if she had any legal handguns registered to her. If she had illegal ones…"You've been helpful."

Carly straightened, looking pleased. "I have? How so?"

"Thank you for your time," Hunter said, putting his hand around Ariel's elbow and leading her away.

As they joined Poppy, he said, "Jason Barba could've gotten one of Carly's hats at the banquet. We need to track him down. And find out exactly why he could be targeting Ariel."

FOURTEEN

Later that evening, Ariel scrubbed dishes to keep her hands busy while her mind raced with the idea that her ex-boyfriend could be the person behind the attacks on her. Why would Jason want to hurt her after all this time? And why try to steal Dash when he had never liked the animals?

Hunter's phone rang and she listened to the one-sided conversation, anything to take her mind off Jason.

"You got him?" he said. "That's good. Put him in the interrogation room."

Ariel's heart stuttered and her gaze swung to Hunter. *Got him? As in Jason?*

"I'll—" Hunter hesitated and glanced toward her. "We'll be there shortly."

She threw down the dish towel and hurried to his side. "What's happening?"

"Brayden found Jason Barba. I want to know what he was doing at the banquet hall last night and if he is the one trying to kill you." Hunter's grim tone sent a shiver down her spine. "We need to go."

Nerves jangling, she swallowed back the emotions clogging her throat. Was this nightmare finally about to end? All the ramifications crowded her mind. Her life could resume. Hunter would leave. But so many questions still bounced around unanswered.

If Jason was the one who was after her, then who was after Lance and Jared? And where was Violet?

Hunter drove them to headquarters. He hoped and prayed to put an end to the threat against Ariel's life tonight. She'd endured so much over the past week, he wanted to let her get back to her normal life. One that didn't include him.

Distress cramped his chest. A reaction he wouldn't have dreamed he'd have considering how much he didn't believe in romance or relationships. But the time spent with Ariel was showing him that maybe some relationships were worth taking a risk on. Was *he* willing to take the risk?

He wasn't sure.

Once inside, Maya and Poppy rushed forward to greet Ariel. He handed her off to the two females and left Juneau with them, knowing his teammates would take good care of Ariel while he was in the interrogation room with Jason Barba.

Brayden met him outside the door. "Barba's not very patient. He's been banging on the doors and on the table. This man has a temper."

Hunter bared his teeth. "Let him show me that temper." Was it anger that had prompted this man to try to hurt Ariel?

Walking into the interrogation room with Brayden on his heels, Hunter caught his first glimpse of Jason Barba. The sandy-blond-haired man glared back at Hunter, his gray eyes hard. He wore a plaid flannel shirt with the sleeves rolled up. Hunter stood towering over the sitting man. Jason started to rise but he held up a hand. "Stay seated," he barked.

Brayden took a stance in the corner, crossing his arms and his ankles. He was there only to observe. Or intervene if Hunter lost his own temper.

He turned the metal chair backward so he could straddle it, folding his arms over the top of the back. "Where were you this morning?" he began.

"Sleeping," Jason answered. "I worked until two a.m."

"Can anyone corroborate your whereabouts?"

"What's going on?" Jason gestured with his chin toward Brayden. "He wouldn't tell me."

Hunter wasn't inclined to enlighten the suspect yet. "Where were you Tuesday evening?"

"Working," Jason said.

"Working where?"

"What does it matter?" The irate man folded his arms across his wide chest. "I'm not saying anything more until you tell me why I'm here."

"It matters because your answer will determine whether or not you'll be sitting in a jail cell for the rest of your life," Hunter ground out.

Jason's face drained of color. "I work for a catering company."

"The same catering company that serviced the regional sled dog award ceremony?" he pressed.

"Yes. So?"

"Sabotaging the backdrop to try to crush your ex-girlfriend is a crime," Hunter bit out.

Jason held up his hands and shook his head. "I knew it. I knew you were going to try to pin that on me. No way, man."

"You were angry when she broke up with you," Hunter stated.

Lip curling, the other man said, "I don't know what story she told you, but I broke up with her. She was way more into her dogs than me. It didn't matter what we were doing, if the dogs needed her she dropped me like a hot potato. I didn't want that kind of relationship. I need somebody who's going to be there for me."

"Did you get rough with her? Want to hurt her?"

Jason frowned. "No way, man. Ariel would have turned loose those dogs of hers on me if I'd touched her. They're very protective of her. They wouldn't let anybody get too close to her."

Funny. Her dogs had let Hunter and Juneau get close to her. Hunter liked the dogs even more now. They were clearly good judges of character. "I want to know everything you did the night of the banquet from the moment you arrived at the banquet hall. In fact, I want to know everything you did that day as they were building the backdrop. Were you there?"

"I was not there building a backdrop. I don't belong in that world. Ariel made that very clear. I didn't even realize what the job for that night was till I got there." Jason fidgeted in his chair. "I couldn't watch her up there accepting her award."

"Where did you go?"

"Out back to have a smoke," he said.

Hunter narrowed his eyes at him. "That's a weak alibi."

"Hey, I wasn't alone," he stated. "You can ask my girlfriend, Sandy."

Girlfriend. Hmm. Interesting. Ariel had mentioned she thought the person who'd tried to strangle her was a woman. Could Jason's girlfriend be the one behind the attacks on Ariel?

"You and Sandy were at the event together. Was she with you all day?"

"For most of it."

"You said you were sleeping this morning." Hunter drummed his fingers on the back to the chair he straddled. "Was Sandy with you?"

"I met her for breakfast before she went to work," Jason said. "What happened this morning?"

Hunter stood. "You better hope nobody saw you backstage because if they did, you're going down."

Sweat dripped down the side of Jason's face. "When can I leave?"

"Not until we talk to Sandy. Write down her full name, phone number and place of employment."

Brayden stepped forward with paper and pen.

Jason jotted down the information and slid the paper across the table to Hunter.

Grabbing the paper, Hunter and Brayden walked out.

"Do you believe him?" Brayden asked.

"Not sure." Was this Sandy person jealous of Ariel? Did she want to eliminate the competition?

Yet that didn't make sense. Ariel and Jason hadn't dated in several years. There was more going on here, and he couldn't see all the moving pieces. Frustration beat a steady rhythm in his head. His gaze went to where Ariel, looking lovely in a long wool skirt and amber-colored sweater, stood talking to Maya, Poppy and Helena. Juneau sat at Ariel's feet. Hunter guessed the other K-9s were in their handlers' offices, which would be where he'd have taken Juneau upon arriving at headquarters if not for Ariel's presence. He turned to Brayden. "Would you be willing to track down Sandy Olsen?"

"I'm on it," his teammate said. "Looks like your lady has made some new friends."

Hunter's face heated. "She's not my lady."

Brayden winked. "Whatever you say." He strode away.

Shaking his head, Hunter joined the women. "Excuse me, I need to talk to Ariel." He drew her to the side while Maya, Poppy and Helena dispersed, going in different directions. "Tell me again who broke up with who?"

"Huh?" Ariel scrunched up her face for a moment. Then her expression cleared. "Oh, you mean with Jason?"

"Yes, with Jason."

"I broke up with him. I told you he was becoming possessive and he didn't like me spending time with the dogs. But he knew when we started dating that the animals are a big part of my life. He wanted me to choose between him or the dogs. Who does that?"

Hunter would never ask Ariel to choose between him and her pack. He pinched the bridge of his nose. Why had his mind even gone there? He was never going to get that far in this relationship with Ariel. He scrubbed a hand over his unshaven jaw. "We should head back to your place."

"What's with Jason? Is he the one?"

"We're still gathering information," he told her. "Until we have a definitive answer, we have to operate with the assumption that the perpetrator is still out there and you're not safe."

Ariel bit her bottom lip, and fear clouded her light brown eyes, emphasizing the gold flecks reflecting the station's fluorescent lights. "As long as you and Juneau are with me, I'll be okay."

Her confidence settled around his heart like a hug. And he prayed he wouldn't let her down.

"Do you mind if we stop for the mail?" Ariel asked Hunter as he turned into her drive. It had been days since she'd thought about the mail, and the bills that were no doubt stacking up. Her dwindling bank account needed a booster, exactly what the race the day after tomorrow would bring if she placed well and received the prize money.

He brought the vehicle to a stop, allowing her to climb out. The box was stuffed full.

Once they were inside the house, she sifted through the mail, and paused to stare at a plain white envelope addressed to her with no return address. Odd...

She opened the letter, pulled out a piece of paper and recognized Violet's flowing handwriting. Her breath hitched. Violet was alive! "Hunter! This is from Violet."

Hunter had changed out of his uniform, opting for worn jeans and a Henley-style T-shirt that made her very aware of the width of his shoulders. He closed the distance between them in a few long strides. "What does it say?"

Ariel swallowed against the trepidation robbing her of her voice.

Please don't let this be a confession.

Her stomach churned and she chastised herself for even going there. Her friend was not guilty of the crimes she was being accused of.

Taking a breath, she read aloud. "'Dear Ariel, I know what people are saying about me. Please believe me, I did not do what the media is telling the world. I didn't kill our tour guide. It was Lance. You have to believe me. I ran, because they were going to kill me, too. Whatever they've told you, it's all lies. You're my best friend. You know me. When it's safe I will return. Love, Violet.'"

Sweet relief lifted the heavy burden off Ariel's shoulders. "See! I told you." Her hands shook as she waved the piece of paper at Hunter. "Violet is innocent. It's Lance and Jared who are lying."

Hunter ran a hand through his dark, thick hair. "She could be just saying that to throw suspicion on them. We won't know the truth until we find her."

Ariel folded the paper and put it back into the envelope. "I don't care what you say. I will not believe that my friend is guilty of these crimes." She blinked back hot tears. "Tomorrow would have been her wedding day."

"Awww, Ariel." Hunter came closer, his nearness sending little shimmers of awareness over her skin.

The temptation to take comfort from him was almost more than she could bear. She stepped into his embrace. Wrapping his arms around her, he rubbed small circles on her back. She laid her cheek against his chest, the steady thump of his heart steadied her. She never wanted this moment to end. Never wanted to leave the safety of his arms. Here, all the fear and stress of the world evaporated.

"I need to bag that letter and envelope as evidence."

His gentle voice was like a hammer to her heart. Her lip curled. She couldn't keep the resentment out of her tone as she pushed away from him and held the letter out to him. "Of course you do. Here."

He held up his hands. "Hold on a second." He snagged a plastic bag from her kitchen drawer. "Slip it in here."

Blowing out a frustrated breath, she carefully slid the envelope containing Violet's letter into the plastic bag. He zipped it closed.

If only she could zip up her growing affection and attraction for this man as easily.

The next morning, Hunter worried about Ariel. Her mood was subdued, and she appeared to be on the verge of tears at any moment as she went about her chores of feeding the dogs, exercising them and cleaning out their kennels. Then she'd gone inside and started baking. The house smelled delicious and his mouth watered as he snagged a couple of oatmeal raisin cookies.

Ariel hardly glanced at him. He wished he could take her pain away. It hurt to see her hurting. But there was nothing he could do.

He set up his laptop at the dining table and was very aware of Ariel puttering around the kitchen. He put in his earbuds as Lorenza gave the team an update for the last week.

The search for Violet was going nowhere. She'd effectively found a place to hide and continued to elude the authorities. Speculation was her wealthy mother was helping her to hide while at the same time demanding law enforcement do everything they could to find her. But so far there was nothing to prove that theory.

Lance and Jared were also in the wind. The location of their "safe house" remained unknown. There had been no communication from the two men.

Meanwhile, Brayden was having trouble tracking down Sandy, Jason's current girlfriend. And the ballistic test done by Tala Ekho came back, showing the weapon used to murder Cal Brooks was not the same gun as the one used to shoot at Ariel. The disparity didn't prove or disprove whether the shooter who'd killed Cal or fired at Ariel here at the property were the same person.

Hunter was surprised when Lorenza gave the floor over to her assistant, Katie Kapowski.

Katie stepped into view of the camera as Hunter's earbuds died. With a grimace, he took them out and lowered the volume on the laptop.

The young woman's red-rimmed eyes tore at Hunter. Something was wrong. Her voice trembled as she said, "Team, I need your help. The Family K Reindeer Sanctuary Ranch, which rescues reindeer, has been robbed."

From the kitchen, Ariel let out a little gasp.

"How can we help?" Helena Maddox asked.

"My aunt is desperate," Katie replied. "A pen of reindeer was set loose. Two are missing. If she loses those reindeer it will devastate the ranch. It's barely functioning as it is. My aunt Addie has pared down to just two ranch hands."

Ariel moved from the kitchen to stand across the table from Hunter, out of view of the computer's camera. She waved to get his attention. He muted his laptop. "Yes?"

"I know Addie Kapowski. You and Juneau could find her reindeer. You found me."

Though Hunter appreciated her confidence in his and Juneau's abilities, he shook his head. "I'm not leaving you."

"Take me with you. I'll be safe with Addie while you two search for the reindeer."

"Not happening."

He unmuted the laptop and heard Lorenza saying, "Hunter, was there something you wanted to share with us? Can you hear me?"

Hunter gritted his teeth. "Sorry, Colonel. I'm at Ariel Potter's house and she—"

Ariel rounded the table and crouched down so that she could be seen in the camera. "Hello, Colonel Gallo. I was saying to Hunter that he and Juneau could find the reindeer. That's what they do, right? Search for missing people, or animals?

I could go with him to see Addie. She probably needs a friend right now. We know each other from church."

Hunter held his breath, waiting to see what Lorenza would say. Several people nodded.

Lorenza nodded, as well. "That's actually a really good idea. I'm going to send you, Hunter. Take Ariel with you. I will also send Poppy because she and Stormy are used to wilderness searches."

Ariel patted Hunter on the shoulder and moved away.

"We're on it, Colonel." He shut his computer down and then stood with his arms folded, waiting for Ariel to return from her bedroom.

When she reappeared, she had on a pair of weatherproof pants and a sweater, wore a beanie on her head, and was carrying a puffy down jacket and gloves. "I'm ready whenever you are."

"Nicely done," he commented wryly.

She smiled. "You're not the only one who can make things happen when they want." She walked past him to scoop up Sasha. "I'll put him in with his mother and meet you at the car."

Hunter had no choice but to follow and was broadsided by the realization he would follow her anywhere.

FIFTEEN

At the Family K Reindeer Sanctuary Ranch, Hunter barely brought the SUV to a halt before Ariel climbed out and strode over the graveled drive toward the front porch of the red-cedar-sided house. Her knock was answered by Addie Kapowski, a tall and imposing woman with short graying brown hair. The older woman drew Ariel in for a quick hug.

Hunter released Juneau from his compartment just as Poppy Walsh arrived. He waited for Poppy and Stormy to join him.

"She has you on a short leash," Poppy commented with a cheeky grin.

He made a face. "Ha ha."

"In all seriousness, Hunter," Poppy said, "we like her."

Hunter's breath caught in his chest, and he shielded his eyes from the winter sun to stare at Poppy. "We?"

"Me, Maya and Helena. Ariel would be good for you."

Though he was glad to know his coworkers approved of Ariel, he needed to set Poppy straight. "There is nothing going on between me and Ariel."

"If you say so." She started walking. "Let's talk to Addie and find her reindeer."

Shaking his head, he grabbed an extra lead from the SUV and strode after his coworker, not liking the way Poppy's comments dug at him. Was he allowing his fondness for Ariel to show? Was he letting his attachment to her cloud his judgment? Was he making a fool of himself like his father had?

Irritated by his own musings, he stopped next to Ariel and Addie on the porch and introduced himself and Poppy.

"Thank you for coming," Addie said. "I've been beside myself. Katie said she'd send help. I hated burdening her with this, but I didn't know what else to do."

"Can you tell us what happened?" Poppy asked.

"Someone let the reindeer loose from the pasture pen where we'd kept them overnight. They are supposed to get their inoculations today," Addie said. "Took a long time, but we managed to corral them into the pen again, but there are still two missing. We can't find either of them. It's been several hours, and I'm worried about poachers."

"Could the gate have been accidentally left unlatched?" Hunter asked.

Addie shook her head. "No. It's a complicated latched system. It must have been deliberately undone by someone who knew the reindeer would be penned up. I fear that one of my ranch hands may have done it."

"Why would you say that?" Ariel asked.

"I had to cut their pay this past winter," Addie explained. She raised a defiant chin. "Times are tough right now. Donations for rescuing injured, orphaned and abused domesticated reindeer have diminished and I'm barely keeping things afloat. And—" she shrugged "—I admit to being short-tempered of late. Gary got the ATV stuck in the mud by the river, which took time and money to get unstuck and I caught Blaze helping himself to my petty cash."

"We'll need to speak to Gary and Blaze," Hunter said. "But first we'll see if we can track down your missing reindeer."

"Do you have anything with the scent of the reindeer on it that we could use for the dogs to sniff out?" Poppy asked.

"Of course. This way." She led them to the reindeer pen.

Hunter kept a casual distance from Ariel but was ready to steady her if she needed. He still wasn't convinced her ankle was completely healed. In fact, he'd seen her slight wince a couple of times when she stepped on the injured foot.

Nearby was a barn where Addie retrieved two leather harnesses. "These belong to the two missing reindeer."

Hunter turned to Ariel. "You and Addie go into the house until we return."

Ariel nodded with a resigned yet understanding smile. "Of course." She threaded her arm through the older woman's. "Let me tell you what's been happening in my life…"

The two women headed back to the house. Hunter kept his gaze on Ariel. He didn't like leaving her unattended. But he was relatively certain she was safe here. He'd been on the lookout for anyone following them from her place and hadn't detected a tail.

Poppy nudged Hunter with her elbow. "Dude, you've got it bad."

"I don't know what you're talking about." He turned his attention to Juneau rather than let Poppy see the truth on his face. He did have it bad and had no idea what to do about it.

Hunter held the harnesses out for the dogs to sniff.

"Find," Hunter instructed Juneau. The dog

lifted his snout to the air, then put it to the ground and took off.

Poppy gave her command to Stormy, as well. The Irish wolfhound let out a bark and raced after Juneau.

"Here we go." Hunter slung the harnesses over his shoulder and hustled alongside Poppy to trail the dogs' paw prints.

They passed a large fenced corral with over twenty horned reindeer milling about, their velvet noses snuffling beneath the snow for vegetation.

In the distance, the sound of the Frontier River drifted on the slight afternoon breeze. Hunter hadn't realized how close the sanctuary was to the multiforked body of water.

The dogs ran down a snow-covered dirt access road and disappeared into the forest surrounding the reindeer sanctuary.

"Look at these." Poppy pointed to tracks in the snow where the access road crossed the property boundary. "Snowshoe prints. And these deep grooves are from the reindeer."

"Not an accident," Hunter remarked. A human wearing snowshoes had released the reindeer. He put a hand on the grip of his sidearm. "Poachers?"

"Could be." Poppy's tone held a grim note.

He was sure she'd seen some horrible treatment of animals as a wildlife trooper in the Kenai Fjord National Park before coming to the K-9 Unit.

Up ahead the dogs barked. Something crashed through the underbrush and trees, coming toward Hunter and Poppy. Man or beast? Hunter braced himself.

A huge reindeer sporting tall antlers rushed at them.

Hunter waved his arms. "Whoa, there, fella."

Poppy mirrored Hunter. The beast skidded to a halt, hot puffs of air coming from his snout, his dark eyes watching them warily as his feet pawed at the ground.

"Easy, boy." He slipped one of the harnesses from his shoulder and cautiously approached the animal. "We don't want to hurt you."

Poppy held out an apple. "Here's a good boy."

The treat seemed to do the trick. The reindeer snuffled her hand and sank his teeth into the apple. While the reindeer was busy chewing, Hunter managed to get the harness slipped over his head and attach the extra lead. He anchored the lead to a nearby tree.

"Good job with the apple," he commented to Poppy.

"I've got carrots, too," she said. "Grabbed them from the barn." She let out a whistle and Stormy came running.

Hunter called out to Juneau. The dog barked in response and raced to his side.

"Let's keep following the snowshoe tracks," Hunter suggested as he leashed up Juneau. "We should keep the dogs close to be safe."

Poppy agreed. They followed the snowshoe tracks to a clearing and a road where there were obvious tire tracks along with reindeer prints that ended where a vehicle was clearly parked.

"It appears as if someone had been intent on taking the two reindeer away but only managed to load up one reindeer," Hunter stated. "We better call this in."

As they collected the reindeer and headed back to the ranch, Poppy used her cell phone to inform the colonel of this development. Lorenza promised to send out a crime scene unit and the Metro police to see if they could trace the tire tracks.

Addie was beside herself when they returned with one of the reindeer in tow.

"I can't tell you how grateful I am," Addie said. "Each reindeer is special. I just hope whoever took my reindeer doesn't destroy him."

"I'm sure the K-9 Unit and the Metro police will do everything they can to find him," Ariel assured her.

Hunter appreciated Ariel's confidence.

Addie patted Ariel's hand. "After hearing what

you've been going through and how well this young man has been taking care of you, I trust you are correct."

Hunter stared at Ariel. What had she told the older woman?

Poppy made a noise suspiciously like a covered laugh. Hunter slanted her a glance, to which she raised her eyebrows, the picture of innocence.

"I hate leaving you here alone," Ariel said. "Maybe I should stay with you."

"I'll stay until Katie can arrive," Poppy offered.

With that settled, Hunter escorted Ariel and Juneau back to the SUV.

"She's a widow, you know," Ariel said as he pulled away from the sanctuary. "She and her husband never had children. Katie is her only relative."

The melancholy note in her tone had Hunter's chest tightening. "It was very kind of you to stay with her while we searched for her reindeer."

Ariel unzipped her jacket. "It was the right thing to do."

"Yes, it was," he agreed. He'd half expected Ariel to insist on searching for the reindeer. His respect and admiration for this woman ratcheted up even more, which made his next words tough to say. "I need to take Violet's letter into headquarters."

Her shoulders drooped and she turned away from him. "Do whatever you have to."

That night after a lasagna dinner, Ariel headed to the kennel building with Hunter and Juneau tagging along. She fed the dogs and turned them out to the exercise yard so she could clean their kennels. Once she and Hunter removed all the beds, toys and dishes, she unwound the water hose to wash down each kennel. They worked well together. Ariel tried not to ruminate on how much she would miss Hunter and Juneau when the time came for them to resume their own lives.

"Let me do that," Hunter said, taking the hose from her hands.

Thankful for his help, she relinquished the hose and moved to grab a large duffel bag from a cupboard. She filled it with the items the dogs would need for the race tomorrow. Ariel had already had Trevor load the sled onto the back of her truck while she and Hunter were at Addie's today. She'd hitch the dog trailer to the truck in the morning.

Hunter turned off the hose and wound it back up. "What are you doing?"

"Prepping for tomorrow." She zipped up the bag. "We'll need to get an early start. I want to be at the race grounds to set up my station before it gets too crowded."

Hunter took her hands in his. "Ariel, I'm sorry but there's no way we can let you go to a race tomorrow. It's too dangerous."

She'd known this was going to be a battle. But she couldn't afford to concede defeat. Sighing, she squeezed his hands. "Hunter, I know it will be dangerous. And I know that every time I step out of the house I could be at risk. But I can't live my life ruled by fear."

A pained expression crossed his handsome features. "Caution. You'd be living your life ruled by *caution*. It's not the same thing."

"I can be cautious. And you'll be there to guarantee my safety just as you were at the banquet." Needing him to understand how important competing in this race was, she said, "The way I make money is by competing in races that allow small teams, and by breeding dogs that are showcased at the races. If I hope to pay Trevor for all that he has been doing around here, I need to finish in the top four slots tomorrow, as well as advertise my next pairing. I also need to line up prospective mushers for my puppies."

He remained silent for a long moment. "Let me run it by Colonel Gallo."

Did he not trust himself to make the call? "I can speak to her. She seems reasonable."

"She is," Hunter said. "I trust her judgment."

"And I trust yours," she told him. She did trust

this man. With her life. And she was beginning to realize she trusted him with her heart. But he wouldn't want to hear that, not now, if ever. He'd made it clear that romance—love—wasn't something he believed in. "Hunter, she put you in charge of protecting me. She obviously considers you the right person for the job. I do, too. You'll protect me."

He didn't look convinced.

Frustrated with him, she said, "I'm going. You're here because I allow it. I don't have to accept your protection or your presence." She put her hand on his chest. His heart beat beneath her palm, solid and strong. Like the man. "Please, don't spoil this for me."

Hunter's gaze held hers, and his blue eyes glinted with an emotion that left her own heart racing.

He covered her hand with his. "What time are we leaving?"

Hunter could tell how excited Ariel was by the prospect of a race. Even the dogs seemed amped as they loaded them in the trailer, their energetic howls bouncing off the metal sides. Since Trevor was going to be coming with them to help Ariel with the dogs, Hunter decided to drive his own vehicle and followed them.

He didn't explain to Ariel the reason he chose

not to ride with her was to make sure that she arrived at the location without mishap. He liked seeing her happy. And he understood how important today was for her business.

Her words about not living her life in fear had struck him at the core.

Too many times he operated out of fear.

He sent up a prayer that Ariel's confidence that nothing would happen today would be fulfilled.

The race venue was twenty miles north of Anchorage. She had explained that this was the last official fun run of the season. Afterward the snow would melt and training would be on dry land.

But thanks to the late spring snowfall, there was still enough of the white stuff on the ground for one last grand finale. She said it would be mostly mushers from the area since the majority of the Iditarod mushers and dogs had already returned to their homes all over the world.

Hunter parked his vehicle in the visitor parking lot, while Ariel drove her truck and trailer through the gate for competitors. He and Juneau hustled to catch up with them. He flashed his badge to the gatekeepers.

It was interesting to watch the way Trevor and Ariel got everything situated, hooking the dogs to the sled in a two-by-two formation. The dogs pranced in place and howled, but they didn't pull against the harnesses, though Hunter could see the muscles rippling in each dog with the effort to keep from prematurely taking off. Ariel slipped a race number over her red down jacket. Once they were ready to take the pack and sled to the start line queue, Ariel handed the young man a stack of flyers.

Hunter caught a glimpse of one that showed a picture of a litter of puppies along with Ariel's name and contact information.

"Make sure everyone gets one of these," she told Trevor.

She turned to Hunter. "Can you walk behind the sled and just keep it steady as we make our way to the start line?"

He was happy to oblige. Thankfully, he'd worn his heavy boots, warm jacket and gloves. He pulled the beanie on his head a little lower over his ears and positioned himself behind the sled. Juneau stayed close, but far enough back not to agitate the sled dogs.

Ariel moved to the front of her line, where Dash and Phoenix were harnessed as the lead dogs. She spoke softly to the dogs and then walked ahead of them. Without hesitation the dogs followed. Meanwhile, Hunter kept a steadying grip on the back bar of the brightly painted yellow sled and walked between the runners, careful not to catch his foot on the ski-like flat boards that would glide over the snow once the team started really pulling. She brought the dogs to a halt and lined up behind three other teams. Then she gave each dog a piece of salmon before joining Hunter at the back of the sled.

The howls of the multiple dogs filled the air along with a few barks by some of the various different breeds being used in the race.

The noise was nearly deafening. Ariel dug in her pocket and brought out two sets of foam earplugs. She handed a set to him and shouted, "It'll make things easier."

Nodding gratefully, he stuffed the little rubbery plugs in his ears, muting the cacophony of sound.

More racers lined up behind them. Hunter counted at least twenty-five teams. He'd never been involved in a race and could see why many enjoyed the adrenaline rush of seeing the dogs and mushers competing to get the best time on the course.

He caught a glimpse of a familiar face in the crowd standing behind the ropes and keeping the spectators from stepping into the path of the dogs.

Carly Winters.

Her gaze was trained on Ariel, and there was such malice in her expression that Hunter's senses went on alert.

He gestured for Ariel to take out an ear plug just as he was doing. When she did, he said, "Is there a reason beyond just the competitive nature of breeders that Carly Winters would want to harm you?"

Ariel drew back with a frown. "No. As I told you, we're not friends. I've only spoken to her when she has asked to buy one of my adult breeding dogs."

Hunter's cell phone vibrated against his chest. It was Helena, his teammate. He motioned to Ariel that he needed to take the call. She nodded. He jogged away from the noise as far as he could while still keeping Ariel in view and held the phone to his ear. "Helena, news?"

"Yes, we found Sandy. She's been in Fairbanks visiting her sister."

"Why didn't Jason tell us where she was going?"

"Apparently it was her way of breaking up with him without having to face him. She decided that the night of the banquet he was still too hung up on Ariel. She left him the same night."

"Hung up enough on her to try to kill her? It doesn't make sense."

"No, it doesn't," Helena agreed. "Hey, another little tidbit. Tala got back to us on that baseball cap you found. There was a long brown hair in the hat, but couldn't get DNA from it or the hat."

Too bad there wasn't a hair follicle to provide DNA. Sandy, Carly and Violet did not have long brown hair. Was there a fourth female suspect?

"It's a synthetic hair."

Surprise gave way to frustration. "A wig."

"Yes."

"So our suspect could be anybody." Irritation fired along his nerves.

"Right. It could've been a man or woman," Helena said.

His gaze sought Carly Winters in the crowd, but she was nowhere to be seen. He needed to find her. "I've a hunch I need to follow. How quickly can you get here? I need someone to watch over Ariel."

"Ten minutes, tops," Helena told him before signing off.

Hunter hung up the phone. He needed to ask Carly some more questions. And time was of the essence because he wasn't going to let anyone hurt Ariel. Just the thought carved through him with the precision of a surgeon's scalpel, cutting away his resistance to allow her into his heart.

SIXTEEN

Ariel placed her feet on the boards along the edge of the sled runners and gripped the handle bar at the back of the sled. The seconds were ticking down. The team in front was amped up, the dogs dancing with excitement as the crowds cheered in anticipation of the start of the last of the season's fun run sled dog races. Teams would deploy in two-minute increments, and the team with the fastest time across the finish line would win. The next teams coming in after the winner would get a percentage of the prize money. Ariel needed that money.

She glanced around, trying to find Hunter among the throng of people gathered to watch. She spied him standing among the crowd, clearly searching for someone. A horn blew. Ariel frowned. It was the sound the judges used to let the mushers know there would be a delay. Like the other mushers, she stepped off her sled, setting the brake that would keep her team in place.

A disembodied voice came through the loud-speakers. "Ariel Potter, please come to the judges' tent ASAP."

Confusion and a prickle of fear slid down her back, creating a shiver that shook her body. She was aware of the gazes of her fellow mushers on her as she waved Trevor over. He had earplugs in but popped them out. "What's going on?"

"I better go find out," Ariel said. "Can you stay with the dogs?"

"Of course." He traded places with her.

Once again, Ariel searched for Hunter. She couldn't see him as she jogged to the official judges' station. Just as she reached the enclosed ten-by-twenty tent, he joined her.

Hunter gave her a questioning look and she shook her head. They entered together. Monitors showing the crowd waiting for the start of the race and displaying the route along the Trozier Track lined one wall of the tent. Video cameras along the trail prevented cheating and alerted EMS if any mushers and their teams had problems.

Ariel took out her earplugs and approached the judging table, where four men and one woman sat. "I'm Ariel Potter."

A gray-haired man with bushy eyebrows steepled his fingers together and stared at her over his thick black-framed glasses. "It's come to our attention, Miss Potter, that you are doping your dogs."

Ariel's jaw went slack. No way could she have heard him correctly. "Excuse me? *Doping?* What on earth are you talking about?"

"We've had a complaint that you are giving your dogs performance-enhancing drugs," the woman at the table said with a disapproving tone.

Dumbfounded by the accusation, Ariel's gaze jumped to Hunter. "I wouldn't ever do something like that."

His troubled blue eyes held hers. "I've seen you giving the dogs some sort of powder in their food."

Disbelief knocked her back a step. "It's vitamins and minerals. Not only is it perfectly legal but good for them." She turned back to the judges. "I do not give my dogs anything to enhance their performance. I would never violate the rules, nor would I put my dogs' health in jeopardy."

"Until that can be verified, you are banned from any races," one of the other male judges stated.

"Banned?" Outrage heated her skin. "This is a fun run."

"It's still a race with a purse."

Ariel's fingers curled at her sides. "This is absurd!"

"The vet will need to take blood samples of your dogs to verify," the woman spoke again. "If the accusation proves false, we will reinstate you."

"Are you serious?" Ariel scoffed. "By the time that happens, the race will be over."

She looked to Hunter for help. He didn't come to her defense. Crushed by his lack of faith in her, she turned on her heels and walked out.

Hunter caught up with her. "Ariel, maybe this is for the best."

"For the best!" She rounded on him. "Did you do this?"

His eyes widened. "No," he said. "Of course not. I would never do that to you."

"Of course not," she mimicked him. "You didn't want me to compete in this race to begin with. Now you've sabotaged me. Thanks, Hunter. I thought I meant more to you than that." She stalked away from him.

"Ariel, where are you going?"

"I'm going to talk with the vet," she called over her shoulder as he walked behind her. "I don't need you with me."

Tears blinded her as her heart caved in on itself. She'd almost considered herself in love with that man. Would she ever learn that was too much of a risk?

* * *

Hunter slowly followed after Ariel, keeping her in sight but giving her enough distance to cool off. It hurt to imagine that she believed he would do something so underhanded. He knew deep in his soul that she was a goodhearted woman who loved her dogs and she would never do anything to hurt them.

But somebody was obviously out to ruin her.

If it wasn't Jason Barba's ex-girlfriend, Sandy, who was in Fairbanks, then that left Jason, Violet James or Carly Winters.

Once Ariel entered the veterinarian's tent, Hunter picked up his pace. When he entered the tent, he found Ariel talking to Dr. Cora Madison. He was surprised to see the K-9 Unit's veterinarian working the race.

Both women stopped talking to stare at him.

He spread his hands wide. "It wasn't me, but I suspect I know who did make the complaint."

"Who?" Ariel's tone was filled with antagonism.

He wasn't ready to divulge his suspicion until he had it confirmed. "I'm going to deal with it. You stay here." He turned to Cora. "Please, don't let her leave this tent. And don't let anyone else in here. Helena is on her way."

Ariel blew out an exasperated breath. "Hunter,

I'm done taking orders from you." She turned away, giving him her back.

A helpless sort of rage infused him. He didn't want her to believe the worst of him. Yet he had questioned her about the supplements she used for the dogs. And he hadn't wanted her to race, but not because of this.

He needed to make this right. He returned to the judges' tent and went to the young man sitting in front of the monitors. After showing his badge, Hunter asked, "Can you pan the crowd?"

"Sure." The man toggled a device on a keyboard sitting on the table in front of him.

Scanning the faces, Hunter didn't see Violet or Carly.

"I need you to send a copy of the last hour of video feed to this person." Hunter took out Eli Partridge's business card. "And then I want you to allow him to tap into the feed so that he can look at the crowd right now. There may be a killer on the loose."

A flash of alarm flared in the younger man's eyes. "You got it."

The gray-haired judge from earlier hurried over. "What are you doing?"

Hunter explained and the gentleman nearly convulsed with panic. The other judges rushed over, obviously realizing that something was going on, and nearly matched the older judge's distress.

"Please, don't make this public," the female judge said.

"Whatever you're going to do, do it quietly," another judge insisted. "We can't have pandemonium. People and dogs will get hurt."

"I'll do my best," Hunter assured them. "Who filed the complaint against Ariel Potter?"

The judges looked at each other.

"It was anonymous," the gray-haired man claimed, his gaze shifting away from Hunter.

Narrowing his eyes, Hunter said, "I don't believe that. If you don't tell me the truth, I'll put an end to this whole race right now."

"You can't do that!" the woman exclaimed. "We're about to start the race."

Hunter ground his teeth together. "Then give me the information I need."

"Just give it to him, Tom," the woman said. "It doesn't matter in the long run."

Tom huffed out an agitated breath. "It was Carly Winters."

Just as Hunter suspected. Ariel's competitor wanted to discredit Ariel and hurt her business. He believed that Carly was behind the attacks on Ariel, as well. Without another word, he hustled out of the tent and nearly mowed over Helena.

"Whoa, slow down," she said, steadying herself. "What gives?"

In rapid-fire words, he gave her the highlights of the situation and where to find Ariel.

Secure that Helena would keep Ariel safe, he ran for his truck.

He was going to have it out with Carly Winters and arrest her for attempted murder.

Ariel's dogs checked out fine, just as she'd known they would. Cora marched off to give the judges an earful, for which Ariel was grateful, but she was too upset to even contemplate joining the race at this point. She wasn't sure why the officials had continued to delay the start of the race...though she suspected it had something to do with Hunter.

Maybe she'd been wrong to accuse him of sabotaging her. But the look in his eyes and his question about the supplements she gave to her dogs had made her see red. And ache with the pain of betrayal.

Just contemplating that Hunter could believe she'd do anything so underhanded and harmful made her insides twist.

And the question of who filed the complaint poked at her like a sharp stick, drawing bits of blood with every stab.

Hunter's questions regarding Carly played

through her head. She'd been truthful that they weren't friends. But she didn't tell him that ever since the other woman had landed in the area and Ariel had refused to sell her a dog, she had made her dislike of Ariel very clear. Was Carly the one behind the complaint? Had the other breeder been so jealous of Ariel's business that she'd tried to hurt her?

A sinking sensation in her abdomen had Ariel needing to grab the nearest chair. Had Carly followed them up the mountain and acted on an opportunity to push her off the cliff? Then, when that attempt on her life hadn't been successful, had the woman tried to steal Dash, Ariel's most sought-after stud? Ariel was sure the person who had tried to strangle her was female or at least sounded like one. Could it have been Carly?

Her competitor had also been at the banquet. She could have easily been the one to orchestrate the collapse of the backdrop.

Heart hammering in her chest, Ariel jumped to her feet. She needed to find Hunter and tell him.

His teammate, Helena, and her partner, a Norwegian elkhound, walked into the tent just as Ariel was rushing out.

Helena's wide green eyes flared with recognition. "Ariel."

She stopped short, glad to see the trooper. "Helena, have you seen Hunter?"

"I just talked to him," she replied. "He left, though. He told me to stay with you and get you back to your place."

"Left?" Disappointment reared, mixed with the anger at his betrayal of trust. "Do you know where he's going?"

"He's following a hunch."

Ariel hesitated. Then determination straightened her spine and infused her muscles with energy. She tugged on Helena's state trooper jacket sleeve, pulling her and her partner into the judges' tent. "I need your help with something. We'll use your badge to get the information I want…"

"I'm here to help you in any way I can," Helena said.

Once inside the tent, Ariel marched up to the judges' table, where the panel sat. "My dogs are fine. But we need some information. Who told you I was doping my dogs?"

One of the judges rolled his eyes. "Not again."

Ariel narrowed her gaze on him. "What do you mean?"

"The other trooper was in here asking the same question," the gray-haired man told her.

Ariel's pulse ticked up. She shared a startled glance with Helena.

Helena stepped forward. "This is official business. What did you tell him?"

The woman sighed. "That the breeder, Carly Winters, was the one who made the accusation."

Helena gasped. "He's headed to Carly's!"

Ariel's breath stalled in her lungs. "I'm afraid she might be dangerous."

Helena's eyebrows dipped. "But just to you, right?"

"We don't know that for sure. She might do anything to keep from being caught." Ariel took her phone out of her jacket pocket. "I'll try to reach Hunter."

Her call went straight to voice mail. She sent a text, as well. Dread gripped Ariel like a harness belted too tightly around her chest. "He's not answering. We have to go to Carly's."

"I'll call for someone to go there," Helena said.

"There's no time. Carly's place isn't far from here," Ariel said. "We have to go ourselves."

"We'll take my rig, but you'll stay in the car."

Not about to argue, Ariel checked with Trevor to make sure he would take the dogs back to her place in the trailer.

With her dogs secure in Trevor's capable hands, Ariel got into Helena's SUV. She sent up a prayer: *Dear Lord, please protect Hunter.*

Hunter arrived at Carly's place, pulling up next to the red truck with the Winters Kennels logo on the side. He studied the house. A curtain moved in an upstairs window.

She was home.

Caution tripped down his spine. He checked his weapon. Then he radioed dispatch, giving them his location and informing them he was questioning a potential suspect in the Potter case.

He climbed from the SUV, keeping an eye on the front of the two-story house. Using the release button on his keychain fob, he released Juneau. The dog jumped out, landing silently on the plowed driveway.

Hunter attached a lead to Juneau's harness, and they approached the front entrance.

As he stepped onto the porch, a strange spitting sound raised the fine hairs at his nape in alarm. Beside him, Juneau let out a howl and then toppled over.

Heart jumping into his throat, Hunter dropped to his knees beside his partner. A blue-and-yellow dart protruded from the dog's side.

A tranquilizer dart.

Anger, swift and dangerous, flowed through Hunter's veins. He plucked the offending thing from Juneau, hoping to keep the full dose of the drug from entering his body. The crunch of footsteps on the porch stairs behind him had him reaching for his sidearm.

"Don't move," a gruff male voice demanded. "Get your hands in the air."

Slowly Hunter raised his hands and swiveled to face Jason Barba. The man held a tranquilizer gun.

"You." Regret for letting the weasel get the drop on him wound around him like an anchor rope to a tree. "Why aren't you still in custody?"

"Lawyer." Jason spit out the word. His face twisted with hatred. "You've gotten in our way far too much."

"Our?" Dread pinched Hunter's gut.

The front door opened and Carly Winters stepped out holding a .32 caliber weapon in her hands. She wore a baseball hat with her kennel logo over a long brown wig.

The pieces of the puzzle shifted. "You two are working together."

"That's right, handsome," Carly said. "Now put your weapon on the ground."

No way was he giving up his sidearm. "Why are you mixed up with Jason? Why are you trying to hurt Ariel?"

"Hey." Jason's voice rose to a higher octave. "What do you mean by mixed up with me?"

"Shut up, Jason," Carly said, her brown eyes glittering with malice. "Trooper, do as you're told or your dog dies." She shifted the barrel of her gun to Juneau.

Afraid she would follow through with her threat and kill his partner, Hunter rushed Carly. He'd rather be shot than let Juneau die.

She screamed and danced back. A sharp pain between his shoulder blades drew Hunter up short. Jason had fired a dart into his back. Another dart hit Hunter in the leg. He dropped to his knees beside his partner.

Carly pushed Hunter over with her foot. "Now, be a good boy and go to sleep."

Hunter fought the drug invading his system as the world went hazy, but it proved to be too strong and he succumbed to the darkness.

SEVENTEEN

With her heart in her throat and fear tingling through her, Ariel held on to the dashboard as Helena drove at a breakneck speed with the siren blaring toward Carly Winters's kennels. The two-story house and outbuilding came into view. There was no sign of Hunter. Carly's truck was not in the driveway, either. Helena brought the SUV to a skidding halt.

Ariel caught sight of a white tail sticking out from beneath the porch.

Dread and panic seized her breath. Juneau!

She sent up a litany of prayers and ignored Helena's directive to stay in the car. Jumping out of the vehicle, Ariel raced to the Siberian husky's side. Helena and her partner, Luna, were right on Ariel's heels. The howls of Carly's dogs inside the building to the side of the house raised the hairs on Ariel's arms.

She dropped to her knees, and her hands were

shaking as she reached out to touch the soft red-and-white fur. "Juneau?"

At the sound of her voice, the dog lifted his head and gave a small howl of distress.

He was alive. Relief brought tears streaming down Ariel's face. "Thank God."

Helena tested the front doorknob. "Locked. We're going to check the back." She and Luna hurried around the house, disappearing from sight.

Ariel tugged Juneau out from beneath the porch, her hands roaming over the dog, looking for injury. But she had a sinking sensation she knew exactly what had happened. He had been tranquilized just as Dash had been the night the intruder tried to steal him.

Carly Winters. She had been the intruder. She was the one behind the attacks on Ariel.

She gathered Juneau's head onto her lap. "You're going to be okay. Where is your handler?"

Ariel's gaze swept the property, looking for any sign of Hunter or Carly. The dogs in the kennel building sounded distressed.

Helena returned. "There's no sign of Hunter or anyone else. The place is empty." She crouched next to Ariel and petted Juneau. "How is he?"

"He'll be okay. He's been drugged. Same thing happened to Dash the other night. Good thing he's a police dog, because taking him would be too risky. Especially once he woke up."

Luna nudged Juneau with her nose.

Helena nodded. "Yes, he'd be aggressive with someone he doesn't know."

"I'm sure Carly plans to dispose of him when she returns." Ariel's heart contracted at the thought.

"Let's get him in the SUV."

Ariel attempted to lift Juneau, but the dog resisted and managed to get his feet under him. He wobbled, and Luna moved to stand next to him. "Juneau must not have been dosed as heavily as Dash."

Helena's gaze went to the kennel building. "I'd better check that out."

"I'll come with you," Ariel said. Hunter could be in there injured. Or worse. Apprehension slithered along her limbs.

Walking at Ariel's side, Juneau let out a series of ear-piercing howls as they approached the building.

"Stay behind me." Helena had Luna sniff the doorknob before she tried it and found it unlocked. She pushed the door open. The howling of the dogs inside their crates was deafening. Ariel peered around Helena. Hunter was nowhere to be seen. But the conditions in which the dogs were living was deplorable.

Horrified, Ariel's stomach rolled. "We have to rescue these dogs. I can't believe that Carly would do this."

"I'll call dispatch," Helena said. "I'll have them alert the humane society."

Ariel couldn't just leave the dogs like this, but her priority had to be finding Hunter. Where was he?

Juneau tried to vocalize something, and the dog's apparent distress broke Ariel's heart. She had no idea what the dog was saying, but she could only guess that he was hurting from the absence of his handler. The same way Ariel was. "I know, boy, we'll find him. I miss Hunter, too."

She more than missed him. She loved him. Deep inside she couldn't deny the truth. Despite his betrayal, despite knowing his stance on love and relationships, she was madly in love with Hunter. She sent up a plea to God that she'd have a chance to tell him.

A Metro police cruiser came screaming down the drive. Ariel was glad to see it was Officer Everett Brand. She and Helena hurried over and filled him in. He promised to alert the department and to stay until someone came to take care of the dogs.

Helena turned to Ariel. "I'll take you and Juneau to your house. It's the safest place for you both."

Ariel didn't want to be left out of the search for Hunter, but she had no say in the matter. So, with a heavy heart, she climbed into the passenger seat of Helena's SUV with Juneau on her lap. He howled, and Ariel rolled down the window. He stuck his head out as Helena drove away from Carly's.

When they passed the turnoff for the Chugach State Park, Juneau's agitation was more than they could contain within the confines of the cab of Helena's SUV. Helena pulled the vehicle to the side of the road. Once they came to a halt, the canine jumped out the window and ran back toward the entrance to the state park.

"He must've caught Hunter's scent," Helena said.

"Follow him!"

The tires threw dirt and snow as Helena made a quick U-turn. Ariel prayed for all she was worth that they reached Hunter in time to prevent whatever Carly had planned.

Hunter came to with a jolt. His eyes opened to a cloudy sky. The sensation of moving made him dizzy. He attempted to sit up, but his body was strapped down. Dropping his chin to see what was going on, he realized he'd been secured to a rescue basket. He craned his neck in an effort to look behind him and could see that Jason and

Carly had attached ropes to the basket and were dragging him up a snowy trail. Flattop Mountain loomed ahead of them. They were taking him to the place where Cal Brooks had died and where Ariel had been pushed off the cliff.

"How much farther?" Jason whined. He sounded breathless with the effort of pulling the basket.

Hunter took grim satisfaction in the fact that the much smaller man was struggling.

"Just keep going," Carly snapped. "I had no idea you were such a wimp."

"Hey," Jason said. "I'm helping you, aren't I?"

Hunter spread his fingers wide, gauging how much movement he could get beneath the straps. A little. Hoping he could reach his SUV key fob and the GPS tracker built into the device, he worked at getting his hands to the front pocket of his pants. Hunter glanced back and met Jason's gaze, just as his fingers closed around the knob. Sending a silent prayer of thanks, he deployed the tracker.

"He's awake!" Jason jerked to a stop, forcing Carly to do the same.

Carly rounded the basket to stand at Hunter's feet. "So he is." She looked up toward where they were going and then back at Hunter. A split second later, she grabbed her gun from the pocket of her jacket. "Undo the straps," she instructed Jason. "He can walk the rest of the way."

Jason undid the buckles.

Hunter pushed himself up onto his elbows. His head swam. The world tilted. He gave himself a shake and sat up higher.

"Get him to his feet," Carly snarled. "I don't have all day. I need to get back to the race and be there at the finish."

Jason pushed Hunter's back. "Get up. You heard her."

Forcing himself, Hunter struggled to stand. He got his feet under him but had to put his hands on his thighs and bend over until the world righted.

"Start moving," Carly said. "We'll get the basket on the way back down."

"Carly, what's your plan?" Hunter's words came out a bit slurred. "You're only making matters worse for yourselves."

"Oh, no, not worse for us," she said. "It's gonna be worse for Ariel."

"That's right," Jason said. "Ariel thinks she's too good for me."

"Too good for *us*," Carly reminded him.

"Uh, sure," Jason agreed.

Hunter struggled to understand. "How do you two know each other?" He glanced back to see them look at each other. "You're planning to kill me anyway, so just tell me the truth."

He prayed a rescue would come long before she pulled that trigger.

Carly snickered. "We met at a sled dog event a few months ago and realized we had a common enemy. Ariel."

"I thought you said you didn't like dogs," Hunter said to Jason.

"I wasn't there to watch the dogs," Jason snapped. "I was with the catering staff. Duh."

"Why do you want to hurt Ariel?" Hunter asked Carly. "Jason, I get, because Ariel dumped him. But you? What did she do to you?"

Jason sputtered. "That's not true. I broke up with her."

Ignoring him, Carly's lips twisted with contempt. "She's been nothing but a pain in my side since I arrived in Anchorage. I have Alaskan Huskies that are just as good as hers. Yet I lost out on selling my most recent litter to people who bought from her instead. Since stealing her prized stud didn't go as planned, I decided with her out of the way, I might be able to acquire some, if not all, of her dogs and expand my operation."

The woman had seriously flawed logic. Ariel's parents would step in and take care of the dogs. Hunter's chest knotted with dread. Best not to point that out or these two might go after Ariel's parents or anyone else who stood in their way. "What do you intend to do to Ariel?"

"It will be ingenious," Jason said. "Carly's got it all figured out. We're gonna push you over the cliff. And then we'll use your gun to kill Ariel."

"Everyone will think you killed her and then threw yourself over the cliff out of guilt," Carly finished.

He didn't point out the error in their plan. First, there was no logical reason why he'd hurt Ariel and second, the medical examiner would know he was dead long before Ariel. Instead, he said, "So you followed Ariel up the mountain and pushed her off the cliff."

"No," Carly said. "But I wish I had."

"Then it was you," Hunter said to Jason.

"No way. I didn't know about that until I saw the nightly news."

"Same here," Carly echoed.

Hunter wasn't sure he believed them, but why would they lie now? "And then you tried to strangle her?"

"Yes, but you got in the way," she said.

Jason snorted.

"You couldn't have done it," Carly sneered at Jason.

"You better watch out," Jason yelled. "Or you might find yourself going over the cliff, too."

Carly waved the gun at him. "Ha. I'm the one who knows how to use a gun."

Concerned the two might start brawling and the gun might go off, Hunter interjected, "You're the one who shot at Ariel."

Narrowing her eyes, Carly said, "Yes. I should've brought my rifle instead of the .32. But I'd heard on the news that the tour guide had been killed with a .32, so I figured if you all thought the same person was shooting at Ariel, I would be in the clear. Now, no more talk. Move it."

As they reached the outcrop, he turned his back to the cliff. Better to make them look him in the eye. "You won't get away with this."

In the distance, a siren echoed through the valley floor. Hunter wanted to cheer, but he wasn't out of danger. He needed to keep these two from doing anything rash until his team reached him.

Hunter couldn't let Carly and Jason off this mountain. He wasn't sure how he would pull it off, but no matter what, he couldn't let them get to Ariel. In that moment, he realized what he had been fighting for so long. He loved her. He'd fallen hopelessly in love with Ariel and wanted to spend the rest of his life with her. But first, he had to figure out a way out of this predicament.

Jason advanced on him.

Hunter braced himself, his heart crying out

to God for help, because he feared the moment would come when he'd have to choose between being shot or pushed over the cliff.

Ariel and Helena and Luna raced after Juneau up the mountain trail, following the footprints in the snow and the deep grooves of something being dragged along the surface. In the distance a siren wailed. But would more officers make a difference? What if Hunter was already injured or dead?

With each passing second, despair threatened to rob Ariel of her strength. Under her breath she prayed for God to show them where to find Hunter before it was too late.

When they came upon the rescue basket abandoned in the middle of the trail, and another set of footprints, Ariel had a jolt of hope that Hunter was still alive.

Helena held a finger to her lips, then whispered, "They can't be too far ahead."

The footprints led toward the outcrop where she'd been sent over the edge. Where all of this had started.

Juneau sniffed the footprints and then dashed ahead with Luna at his side. Ariel and Helena picked up speed.

Voices drifted on the afternoon breeze.

Adrenaline flooding her veins, Ariel grabbed

Helena by the arm and crouched down behind a bramble bush. Juneau came bounding back to Ariel, while Luna appeared next to Helena. The trooper motioned she would head off to the right and circle around.

Grabbing Juneau by the collar, Ariel slowly and as stealthily as she could moved forward until she was in a position to see that Jason and Carly had Hunter backed up to the edge of the cliff.

Jason and Carly were working together? Carly had a gun in her hand.

Mind. Blowing. It took all of Ariel's self-control not to cry out with rage and fear. Juneau lunged forward, but she held him back, afraid Carly would shoot him. Ariel pointed to the ground, hoping Juneau would understand. He folded down onto his belly. She had to figure out a way to save Hunter. Or at least buy enough time for Helena to get into place.

She rose to her feet, intending to distract Jason and Carly. Her gaze collided with Hunter's.

His eyes widened and he gave a subtle shake of his head. To Jason and Carly he said, "You need to reconsider your plan. This won't work. You're going to get caught."

Beside her, Juneau belly-crawled forward, closer and closer to Jason and Carly. Ariel searched for something to use as a distraction and grabbed a large stone. Using all her strength, she lobbed the rock off to the left of Jason. He took the bait, spinning away from Carly and Hunter, looking for the source of the noise.

Carly, however, turned around to face Ariel. She aimed the gun at her. "Well, this will make things easier."

Hunter shouted, "Attack!"

Juneau sprang up like his legs were made of springs and propelled himself at Carly, latching onto her arm. At the same moment, Hunter tackled the woman from behind, sending her flying forward.

Jason whirled around and charged at Ariel. But a streak of gray and white drove at him. Luna's paws landed on Jason's chest and the dog pushed him back. Jason fell onto his backside.

Helena rushed out of the trees. "State Trooper, put your hands up!"

Hunter quickly handcuffed Carly and recited the vile woman her Miranda rights while Helena did the same with Jason. The two dogs stood guard, baring their teeth. Juneau let out a howl that reverberated across the mountain.

Ariel's legs wouldn't hold her. She sank onto the ground. Then Hunter was at her side. He gathered her into his arms, and as she clung to him, her whole body shook with an overwhelming sense of relief.

And love.

He held her close. "It's okay. We're all okay now."

"Let's get these two down the mountain," Helena said.

Hunter helped Ariel to her feet, then gripped her biceps and looked her in the eye. "Those two will never bother you again, Ariel."

She nodded, thankful that the nightmare with Carly and Jason had ended, and yet what did the future hold? What about Violet?

By the time they got down to the bottom of the mountain, the whole K-9 Unit had assembled along with several Metro PD officers. Colonel Lorenza Gallo stepped forward, directing everyone.

Officer Everett Brand took Carly Winters into custody, placing her into his cruiser, and Officer Gorman followed suit with Jason.

Once the two suspects were headed to jail, Lorenza turned to Hunter. "Did they tell you what happened to Violet James?"

Hunter shook his head with frustration. "Carly and Jason say they had nothing to do with what happened on the mountain. They claim they heard about Ariel's fall on the news, which gave the two of them the idea of trying to do away with her once and for all."

He sent up a silent praise that Carly and Jason hadn't succeeded. His heart still jolted every time he relived that moment when Ariel rose up from behind the bushes. It was a gutsy move that had him terrified that Carly would kill her. But thankfully, his partner, and his coworker, had been heroes, taking down the villains.

The colonel's lips twisted with annoyance. "I was hoping this would all be tied up in a neat bow. And these two would have revealed what happened." She gazed up the mountain in question. "We have to keep working this case, people." She turned around and looked at her team. "All right, everyone back to work. Find Violet James, Lance Wells and Jared Dennis." To Hunter, she said, "I'm glad you're safe. I wouldn't want to lose you."

Hunter tucked her words away, grateful to work for such a great boss.

Lorenza then moved away to talk to Helena. Judging from the expression on his teammate's face, she was pleased with their boss's praise.

Poppy and Maya had taken Ariel off to the side.

Gabriel, Sean, Will and Brayden, along with their respective dogs, crowded around Hunter.

"Man, that was close," Brayden said.

"You're telling me," Hunter replied. "If it weren't for Ariel and Helena." His gaze went to Ariel. Juneau was plastered to her side. After making sure Hunter was intact, the dog had stuck close to Ariel. And that was exactly where Hunter wanted to be.

He looked back at his friends and coworkers. "Would one of you give me and Ariel a ride back to her place?"

"I'll be giving you a ride back," Gabriel said. "But it seems Ariel already has a ride."

Hunter turned to see that Ariel and Juneau were following Poppy to her rig.

He gave a whistle, bringing Juneau back to his side. "If you wouldn't mind, I'd like to stop at my place. A change of clothes is in order." His uniform was sopping wet and muddy and gross, not the way he wanted to look when he confessed to Ariel he loved her.

That night Ariel sat on the back porch with Sasha on her lap. She'd let the dogs out in the fenced yard, and their happy howling as they had fun after their last feeding for the day made her smile. She lamented she hadn't made any money at the race, but she was so thankful she'd been able to save Hunter.

She loved him more than she'd believed possible. When would she see him again? Would it be too brazen of her to call him and ask him to come over?

Doubt swamped her. Not only did he think her capable of doping her dogs, he didn't believe in love. How could they have a future together?

Perhaps it was best for her to suffer her wounded heart alone.

In the twilight of evening, a car turned off the main road onto the snow-packed driveway. Her pulse skipped a beat, then raced through her veins.

Hunter.

His SUV came to a halt. Juneau's plaintive howling reached Ariel, and she smiled. The back compartment opened. Juneau jumped out and raced to her. She held her arms wide, mindful of Sasha sitting on her knees. Juneau skidded to a halt, his rough tongue licking her face.

Her gaze went to Hunter. He walked toward her, looking so handsome in khakis and a leather bomber jacket. His piercing blue eyes held hers. "May I join you?"

She scooted over to make room for him to sit on the back porch. He scrubbed Sasha behind the ears, then took the puppy and set him on the ground. Ariel tucked in her chin. What was this about?

He gathered her hands in his. "I can't believe you saved my life today."

Her anger resurfacing, she shot back, "But you could believe I'd dope my dogs?"

"The minute you explained what the powder was, I realized I was wrong not to come to your defense." He squeezed her hands. "I'm sorry. Please forgive me."

Her anger left in a rush. He was a cop. It was his job to be suspicious, after all. "I understand. I forgive you."

"What you did today was very dangerous."

"What was it you said to me? That I have to trust that God will keep us safe?"

His mouth quirked. "I did say that. And I do believe it. And I believe in you."

She drew back, not sure what to make of his words. "Since when?"

He lifted her hands and kissed her knuckles. "Since the first time I laid eyes on you."

A short laugh escaped her. "Now, I know that's not true. The first time you saw me, I was lying facedown in a bramble bush."

His deep-throated laugh made her giddy. "Okay, maybe not the first time I saw you. But not too long after that. You looked at me with such trust in your eyes. I've never had anyone put that kind of faith in me."

"I do trust you, Hunter. More than you could possibly know." She took a breath. This could be the only opportunity she had to say it. She was going to dig deep and find the courage to take the risk. "I love you. I know that probably scares you. You don't believe in love—"

He put a finger to her lips, cutting her off. "No, Ariel, that doesn't scare me. Not anymore. You taught me that love doesn't have to be a risk. It doesn't have to be scary. Love can be beautiful."

Delight and hope blossomed in her chest. "Do you mean that?"

"I do," he said. "I love you, too, Ariel Potter. And I hope to spend the rest of my life with you, by your side. If you'll have me and Juneau."

Elated beyond measure, she practically shouted, "Of course."

She tugged her hands from his and threw her arms around his neck. "Kiss me," she pleaded.

"I'll kiss you every moment possible," he promised.

And he kissed her.

* * * * *

*Look for the next book in the
Alaska K-9 Unit series, Poppy Walsh's story,*
Wilderness Defender
by Maggie K. Black, available in May 2021.

*ALASKA K-9 UNIT
These state troopers fight for justice with the
help of their brave canine partners.*

Dear Reader,

Alaska. When I think of the northern state, I think of wide-open spaces, snow and beauty mixed with wild terrain. A perfect setting for a suspense story. Last summer when my editor talked about the next continuity being set in Alaska with Alaska State Troopers and K-9 dogs, I got very excited to think about all the research that I would need to do, never realizing that I would be asked to start our continuity off.

Setting up a continuity is always a challenge and a pleasure. There are so many moving parts to keep track of, but ultimately, the story comes down to two characters facing life-and-death choices and finding love.

For Ariel Potter, growing up with nomadic parents left her feeling a little out of step with the rest of the world. Because she hadn't made deep bonds in those formative years, she yearned for love but was held back by fear. Alaska State Trooper and K-9 handler Hunter McCord viewed love as a risk he wasn't willing to take. But protecting Ariel from those who wanted to harm her forced Hunter to reassess his opinion of love and romance. And Ariel discovered that letting go of fear meant trusting God to keep her safe. Together, with their faith in God, Ariel and Hunter, along with Hunter's K-9 partner, Juneau, managed to thwart those who wanted to hurt Ariel. In the process, they discovered that love, when it's right and true, is beautiful and worth risking everything.

I hope you will continue on with us in the journey through the Alaska K-9 Unit as each book will come closer and closer to discovering what happened that day on the mountain.

Until we meet again,
Terri Reed

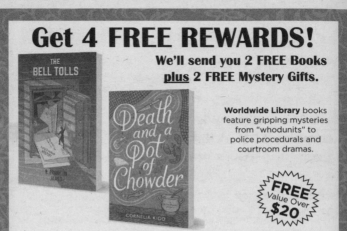